HOW TO AVOID DEATH ON A DAILY BASIS

Book One
Welcome to Probet
by
V. Moody

Cover Artist: Erick Efata

TABLE OF CONTENTS

1. Where Are We?

The first thing I saw was the sky. I closed my eyes again. I remembered coming home after another crappy day at work, heating a frozen lasagne in the microwave — it tasted like cardboard — and falling into bed. The ceiling of my bedroom was what should have been hanging over me, not a clear blue sky. Not unless a storm had ripped the roof off my building.

My fingers dug into earth and grass scratched at my neck and bare legs. The drone of an insect buzzed past, followed by a distant roar that King Kong would have been proud of.

I sat bolt upright and looked around. Trees surrounded a grassy clearing full of wildflowers. I was in the tee shirt and boxers I had gone to bed in, but there was no bed and my bedroom had a totally different decor.

Something howled from the opposite direction to the roar. The thing that howled sounded closer than the thing that roared. I didn't fancy meeting either.

More heads popped up in the long grass. I got to my feet and saw a dozen or so other people sitting up and looking confused. They all appeared to be close to my age and, like me, dressed for bed. About half were girls.

As people started to get to their feet I realised there were even more than my original estimation. Maybe twenty. They started asking each other questions.

"What's going on?"

"Did anyone else hear that?"

"Where is this?"

"Does anybody know what happened?"

"How did we get here?"

Lots of questions. No answers.

Something buzzed at my ear and I turned sharply to avoid being stung. The thing I reacted to hovered level with my face. It resembled a dragonfly in size, and in every other respect a tiny person with wings. It hissed and bared its fangs at me before zipping off at speed.

My legs folded under me and I fell on all fours. My breathing turned to high pitched wheezing until it ceased altogether. I rolled onto my back and opened and closed my mouth, but air refused to enter.

A face appeared above me. My eyes had watered up, blurring everything. The face belonged to a girl with long, dark hair, but the only other feature I could make out was her freckled nose.

"Hey. Are you okay? Take a breath."

If I could take a breath I would, I wanted to say. But you need air to make words, and I didn't have any.

Just when I thought my lungs were about to explode, my chest relaxed and air rushed in. My gasps sounded like a baby seal calling for its mother.

The girl stood up and backed away, obviously freaked out by me.

I raised a hand, trying to say I was okay. She seemed to understand and looked over to where the others were gathering and started edging towards them. I didn't blame her for not wanting to be left looking after the retarded kid.

Still shaken and breathing hard, I got to my feet. I hadn't had a panic attack since I was twelve. For most people, you feel scared, nervous, shy, you eventually get over it. You tell yourself to stop being silly, and you take the plunge. Learning to swim, asking a girl out, killing a spider — whatever it is, if you can overcome the fear in your mind, you can do it.

That doesn't work if no matter how much you convince your brain to play ball, your body says, "Fuck you," and shuts itself down, leaving you flopping around like a spaz.

It's the reason my life turned out the way it did. The best way to avoid embarrassing myself was to avoid situations that might trigger me. Which meant avoiding people in general. Not great, but manageable. And suddenly I'm stuck with a bunch of strangers in a place, judging by that thing I saw, that isn't even—

"Hey guys, listen up."

The speaker was a tall, blond guy. Ripped, good-looking, your basic alpha male. He was wearing a tee shirt for a band so cool I'd never heard of them, and knee-length shorts. He looked ready for a trip to the beach and maybe a little surfing. Girls and guys alike huddled around him.

"Obviously we aren't in Kansas any more."

I wouldn't have put it in quite such a clichéd way, but he wasn't wrong. Judging by the weird creature I saw earlier, we weren't even on planet Earth any more.

"It's pretty clear none of us knows what's going on, but the important thing is to stay calm. There doesn't appear to be any immediate danger, so sit tight and a few of us will scope out the surroundings, see if we can get our bearings. That cool with everyone?"

A general murmur of assent spread through the crowd, but I expect they would have agreed to form a circle and do the hokey-pokey if Golden Boy had asked them to. By the way, I wasn't jealous or resentful of his ability to wow with a smile and wink. Good for him. I'd long ago given up on any hope of that kind of popularity, and if he could get us out of this place, go, go, Team Golden Boy.

"And, girls," said a guy who had taken up position on Golden Boy's shoulder, "any of you feeling scared, come see me. I'll make you feel safe." He was a black guy with a shaved head and a dazzling smile, wearing a tight vest that showed off his incredibly muscular arms.

"Me first," said a female voice in the crowd, to much tittering.

"Hey, shouldn't we start a fire or something? In case they send out search parties. The smoke will be seen from the air."

Rather than getting on with Golden Boy's plan, suddenly everyone wanted to make a suggestion based on an episode of Bear Grylls they half remembered watching or something equally inane. They seemed to have totally forgotten about the strange noises we'd heard. Having seen the weird fairy creature, I suspected it wasn't just a couple of stray dogs out there. The quicker we found a path or track leading somewhere safe, the better.

Once I got my breath back, I moved closer to the trees, trying to see through the gloomy gaps between gnarly tree trunks. Which was when I saw the group of men headed in our direction, dressed in armour and carrying swords.

2. Welcoming Committee

The armour worn by the approaching men wasn't exactly Roman legionary level, but not far off.

"I think someone's coming." No one heard me, even though I said it quite loud. No surprise. I turned around and cupped my hands around my mouth. "Oi! Company." I jerked a thumb towards the trees behind me.

Having got their attention, the others all swarmed towards me. And then past me.

As they all rushed to see who was coming, I noticed how many of the girls were dressed in skimpy outfits. Possibly a strange time to be checking out the ladies, what with potential murderers about to hack us all to death, but everyone deserves a last meal. The pretty, dark-haired girl who helped me earlier wore a particularly cute silky number. She hurried past, taking great care not to look in my direction.

The last of the stragglers was a black guy who really stood out from the crowd. He had an untidy afro, teeth that didn't seem to fit in his mouth, and he was wearing a onesie decorated with characters from the movie *Batman*, the Tim Burton one. Fair play to him, he was dressed for both comfort and warmth. He even had his feet covered, which would help if we had to make a run for it.

He squinted as he stumbled towards me. I swiftly turned and chased after the others. Just as Pretty Girl didn't want to get stuck with me, I didn't want to get stuck with him.

I only took a few steps before the crowd started backing into me. The men in the trees had emerged. There was one leader, identifiable by his superior armour and flashier sword, followed by six men carrying swords without fancy engravings on their blades, which looked very sharp nonetheless.

"Please remain calm," said the leader. "I am Captain Lari Grayson. I'm here to help."

I could understand what he was saying, but for some reason it didn't feel like English. If I stared at his lips as he spoke, the words didn't quite fit. But this made it harder to listen to what he was saying, so I decided to concentrate on that instead.

"The first thing we need to do is get moving. It's about an hour's walk to town, and then we'll get you some clothes and food." And there was no accent, just a neutral tone.

Nervous muttering started to spread.

"Where are we?"

"Why are we here?"

"What's going on?"

From their voices the other people seemed to be British, with accents ranging from north to south.

"I know you all have questions, and I'll be happy to answer them once we get back, but it isn't safe to stay here. Nothing my men can't handle, but it would be better to avoid trouble. There's more of you than we were expecting, so it's important we stick together. If we are attacked, don't panic and run off. And don't try to help. Just stay behind us, we'll take care of it."

"Attacked? What does that mean?"

"Attacked by who?"

"What the hell are you talking about?"

All excellent questions, and more than adequately answered by the huge monster that burst into the clearing, smashing through the trees with a deafening roar.

The girls started screaming. Some of the boys joined them. One of those boys might have been me.

The thing was huge, more than twice as tall as a human. It had a hairy, ape-like body and a neanderthal type of face. But definitely the face of a person, not an animal. Something about it felt familiar, but it wasn't until a soldier called out, "Ogre!" that the pieces fell into place.

Hearing that word put everything together for me in one mind-blowing moment of clarity. I knew where I was. The fairy, the ogre, the soldiers with swords... this was an RPG.

I had played dozens of similar video games, I recognised all the classic tropes of a fantasy setting, but these weren't computer graphics. I hadn't tried Oculus Rift, or any of the latest virtual reality devices, but I was pretty sure they hadn't got to this stage yet. Everything, from the grass under my feet to the clouds in the sky not only looked like the real thing, I felt the wind against my skin and smelled the musty scent of plants and trees.

The ogre, a classic RPG mob, didn't quite match what I'd expect in game, but it was close enough. A large humanoid creature that looked primitive and angry. It roared and lunged, pounding the ground with its gigantic fists.

The soldiers formed a semicircle around the ogre, waving and shouting at it. If it moved to attack one of them, a soldier on the other side would start calling it.

"Hey, dummy. Over here! Over here!"

Spoilt for choice, the stupid thing looked this way and that trying to decide who to kill first. And then Captain Grayson appeared on the creature's shoulder.

How he got up there, and how he did it without the ogre noticing, I have no idea, but by the time it realised, the Captain had his sword plunged into its tree-trunk-like neck.

The ogre's scream was even more terrifying than its roar, and a geyser of blood shot into the air. Plenty of screams were added to the mix from the people behind me. I realised while I watched the fight unfold like a cut-scene in a game, the others had all sensibly retreated to the other end of the clearing. But I couldn't accept what I was seeing was real and just stood there.

Captain Grayson clung onto his embedded sword as the ogre thrashed about trying to grab him, but ended up spinning in circles like a dog chasing its tail. Blood sprayed in all directions. I jumped back to avoid getting covered in it.

The ogre slowed and finally collapsed, first to its knees, then flat on its face. Its last act was to loudly evacuate its bowels, ejecting a mass of green-black sludge that filled the air with a disgusting stink they'll never be able to recreate at your local IMAX.

I walked closer to the dead monster and reached out to touch it, wanting to prove to myself it was some kind of hologram. It couldn't possibly be real.

"Don't," said Grayson as he rolled off its back and wiped his sword on the grass. "They sometimes carry diseases."

I snatched back my extended hand. The last thing I wanted was to take damage from some random debuff. I was even starting to think like I was in a game.

3. Player One Ready?

Some people had sunk to their knees, others were in tears. The soldiers, who acted like this was just another day at the office, quickly got everyone up, barking orders at those still in a daze to snap them out of it.

"We have to move," called out Captain Grayson. "The corpse will attract scavengers. We don't want to be here when that happens."

Slowly the shock wore off, and we formed a vague line. With the soldiers on either side of us, we set off through the trees.

Nobody said anything as we all concentrated on working our way in between the densely populated trees, keeping an eye open for further attacks. Without shoes it took all your attention to avoid stepping on something painful. *Ohs* and *ahs* and *shits* rang out as people hopped around clutching their feet. Met by shushing from those fearful of drawing the attention of more monsters.

I was too excited to be scared. If this really was a game, would you have to collect experience points to level up?

Perhaps we'd be able to gain abilities and skills.

Was there a status screen to show us our stats and hit points?

I stopped and started slapping the air in front of me, trying to trigger some kind of user interface. I had hoped a futuristic HUD would appear, but nothing happened. I stood there trying different combinations of invisible button pushing like an epileptic body-popper. People walked past giving me odd looks until one of the soldiers nudged me to keep moving.

An hour later, we emerged into a meadow of wildflowers. I half expected to look up and see two suns or a floating city, but the sky was blue and the clouds were white. A normal summer's day, warm and mild.

A few minutes after that we came to a fence, beyond which crops grew in large fields. Wheat or something similar as far as I could tell. In the distance stood buildings, maybe a dozen or so. It took us another hour of trudging around the edge of the field to finally arrive in town, although it more resembled a small village. A sign probably said the name of the place, but it was in a weird script I couldn't read or even recognise.

Our escort led us to a large hut. We went around the outskirts so didn't get a chance to see the town or its inhabitants properly, although there were banging noises coming from somewhere and weird smells I couldn't identify.

Inside the hut were rows of benches. People sat down and immediately started complaining. The soldiers came round with a pail of water and a small cup we had to share. We were also given a bun that tasted sweet. It wasn't bad. Then we were shown where the toilets were, and a mad rush followed.

I didn't need to go, so I stayed sitting on one end of a bench and looked around the room. Apart from the benches, there was a desk and what looked like a map on the wall. Some boxes stacked next to the desk seemed to be full of clothes.

People returned from the bathrooms looking unhappy. Most RPG games didn't take their realism all the way to needing toilet breaks, but I assumed facilities would be on the basic side. A hole in the ground, even.

As I tried to look for clues as to what kind of world this was and what it required from me, someone sat next to me. I turned to find the squinty black guy with the Batman onesie. I wondered if he was even a real person. If I really had become part of an advanced virtual reality game without knowing it, these people could all be computer-controlled NPCs.

Then again, who would program a character to look like this? Clearly he was another player, and judging by his appearance, maybe a huge nerd. He might actually be better at these sorts of games than me.

"Hey," he said, "it's like we're inside some kind of computer game, isn't it. My name's Maurice, by the way."

"Colin," I said with a nod. "So, are you good at video games?"

"Can't stand 'em. I'm a board game purist, myself."

Turned out he was such a huge nerd, even in the age of nerd empowerment, he ranked as totally useless.

Captain Grayson stood at the front, leaning on his desk like the cool teacher at school, only better armed, although I guess that depends on what kind of school you went to. He waited until everyone was back from the loo before straightening up and slapping his hands together.

"Right. First things first, you'll be wanting to know where you are, how you got here, and why. That's the big one, right? So, this town you're in is called Probet. It's in a country called Flatland, because it's very flat."

He raised his eyebrows like he'd revealed a valuable secret. When he got no response, he turned and pointed at the map behind him.

"We're this bit in the middle. Nothing much here but farmland and forests. These are the four major cities." He pointed to circular marks at the top, bottom, left and right of the map. "We can go into more about them later."

He faced front again and folded his arms and took in a deep breath like he wasn't looking forward to telling us the next part and needed to prepare himself. The room hushed in anticipation.

"As for how you got here and why, nobody really knows."

A wave of grumbling and muttering washed over the unhappy audience.

"I know, it's not what you wanted to hear, but that's how it is. For the last century, every leap year, on the longest day of high summer, a group of young people appear in the glen where you woke up. Sometimes it's three or four, sometimes, as in this case, it's many more. These people are destined for greatness. If they can survive, that is. I won't sugarcoat the truth for you, this is a hard land to live in, even for those of us born here. There are many things that will try to kill you. But if you can adapt, there are also great rewards that you can claim. Some of those who came before you have become legends."

He sat back on the corner off the desk, very much giving off an impression of mission accomplished.

Golden Boy stood up a few rows behind me and spoke in a loud, irritated voice. "I don't know what the fuck you're talking about, but we want to go home. Now. If you're not going to tell us what's really going on, give me a phone."

"Don't be such a dick," said another guy. This one had a highly-groomed beard and a short back and sides so severe it must have been sculpted with a chisel. He didn't have a top on and a sleeve tattoo covered his right arm. "Obviously they don't have phones here. Did you not see that thing out there? I want answers just as much as you, bruv, but we ain't going home any time soon, I can tell you that much."

"You're the dick, mate," Golden Boy shot back. "Can't you tell we're being pranked? Probably cameras all over this place. Everyone's having a good laugh at us, ha, ha, ha. Well fuck that. I've got better things to do than provide entertainment for free."

The two alphas continued to snap at each other as

more people joined in the pointless debate. I noticed Captain Grayson yawning. He had a 'seen it all before' expression on his face and seemed in no hurry to intervene.

"Just stop for a second," said one of the girls, practically shrieking in order to get everyone's attention. She was tall and athletic-looking, with straight brown hair in a bob, although her oversized white tee shirt made it hard to get a proper idea of her figure. Not that I was looking. "This is getting us nowhere. Let's at least hear him out." She turned to Grayson. "What is it we're expected to do here?"

"Ah, okay," said Grayson. "First we need to get you some clothes. Then each of you will be given a weapon. We only have a limited selection, but they'll do for now. We'll feed you for the next three days, but after that you'll be expected to provide for yourselves, same as everybody else."

"Provide for ourselves how?" asked the girl.

"There's only one way," said Grayson. "By killing monsters."

"I'm a student, for God's sake," screamed the girl. "I don't know how to kill monsters."

"Now, now, don't get hysterical," said Captain Grayson, which is never a good thing to say to a hysterical woman. "Nobody expects you to hunt down ogres and wyverns. There are plenty of smaller, less dangerous beasts that I'm sure you'll be able to handle."

"I don't care," the girl said in the same high-pitched shriek. "I don't want to kill anything! I'm not a murderer."

This was met by a chorus of agreement from the girls sat beside her.

"I'm sorry," said Captain Grayson, "but this land is overrun with monsters. It's just a fact of life here. You don't have to kill them if you don't want to, but they certainly will try to kill you. We don't call them monsters for nothing. Even if you don't plan on hunting, you need to be able to defend yourselves. That's why I'm going to give you each a weapon."

He signalled two of his men who had appeared in the doorway, carrying an assortment of weapons, which they handed out randomly.

"These aren't all that great, but they're all we have. Feel free to swap them among yourselves if you want."

There was more grumbling as the type of weapon each person received varied greatly. And I mean *greatly*.

People who received small swords, daggers and machetes seemed pleased. The ones who got handed sticks, metal rods and rocks attached to a bit of wood, less so. One guy got a whip — which looked cool but not that practical — and I saw a girl look horrified as a spiked ball was thrust at her. It wasn't attached to anything, just a ball with spikes.

I was one of the people to get a stick. I think they had run out of real weapons and somebody had gone out and dug up a fence or something so we'd all have something. It was a bit like a baseball bat, so it could probably do a bit of damage, assuming it didn't break in half.

Maurice got a metal rod, about the size of a fire poker. It was too thin to do any serious damage, but if he sharpened the end, he could probably take someone's eye out.

Once everyone had their weapon, the trading started. Or at least, attempted trading. It was pretty obvious which weapons were better, and everyone wanted to trade up, not down. Arguments broke out, and now that everyone was armed, things felt quite scary. The soldiers stepped in and pushed people back into their seats.

"I know this isn't ideal," said Grayson, "but you will very quickly be able to get yourself something better. Don't get hung up on anything right now, it's all temporary." He smiled with such confidence and lack of concern, it made me think things weren't going to be so bad.

If this really was a game, a crappy weapon to start off with would be normal. I'd soon find a decent sword or axe or something. In the meantime, I needed to figure out the rules and how best to exploit them. Farming, grinding, doing simple quests — there had to be plenty of ways to level up fast.

I could do that stuff, maybe even do it better than some of these six-foot meatbags. I had quite a good feeling about the future.

"Have some faith in yourselves," said Grayson, still smiling. "Looking at all of you young, healthy boys and girls, I'm confident at least one in three of you will make it."

Which meant he expected two-thirds of us to die. If this wasn't a game... The good feeling went away.

4. F.A.Q.

"Any questions?"

For the next few minutes, Grayson fielded a barrage of different questions.

"Is there a way for us to go home?"

"Not right now. But that's not to say there's isn't a way that hasn't been found yet. You may be the one who discovers it."

"You said there were others before us. Where are they? Can we talk to them?"

"They've all moved on, mostly to one of the big cities. If you meet one of them, I'm sure they'll be happy to talk to you."

"Is this a game?"

"No. I assure you this is not a game."

"Can we die?"

"Yes."

"If we die, can we come back to life?"

Grayson pulled a face. "Well, there are healers who can treat severe injuries, but once you're dead, you're dead, as far as I know."

"Are you sure this isn't a game?"

"I'm very sure."

"Does magic exist here?"

"Yes." This sent a buzz around the room as people got excited. "But it's very rare, and people who can actually put it to good use are even rarer. Most blow off their own hands the first time they try it."

"What about dragons? Do they exist?"

"I've never seen one myself, but there are those who claim to have encountered them."

"This is definitely a game, isn't it?"

Grayson put his hand on his hips and looked directly at me. "For the last time, this isn't a game. Please stop asking that."

After that, most of the questions got the same sort of answers — *I don't know. You'll have to figure that out for yourself. I'm not sure* — until they petered out and we sat there staring at him.

"Is that it?" said Grayson. "All right, then. Next thing we need to do is get you some clothes. You can't walk around looking like that!"

Grayson bent down and dragged out the boxes next to the desk. There were four of them, and they were each overflowing with shirts and trousers.

"These aren't particularly stylish, but they will do until you can buy something more to your liking. Take whatever fits, it's all free."

People started walking over to have a rummage. I noticed another couple of boxes by the wall which had footwear in them. While a crowd formed around the clothes, I made for the shoes. The walk to town had been a painful one, and finding a pair of shoes that fit seemed much more important than a matching top and bottom ensemble.

Maurice peered over my shoulder as I tried to find something that looked sturdy. They were all old and used, mostly sandals and cloth slippers, but I dug out a pair of strappy boots that covered my foot and ankle. Not the greatest fit, but they didn't fall off. Maurice grabbed sandals with one clasp broken.

By the time we got to have a look in the clothing boxes, the only things left looked more like rags. The others had put on their new gear, and none of it looked ready for the catwalk. The material was coarse, and everything leaned towards baggy.

The shirt I decided on was a sack with holes for head

and arms. It had a slash across the stomach with red-brown stains around it. The bottom of the trousers hung around my calves, and the waist was many sizes too big. But the material was thick, and some string would sort out the waist. Until then I'd have to hold it up with my hands. Looking at the stuff in the boxes, I got the impression these had all come from our predecessors who had met with sticky ends. Pretty much everyone's clothes had rips and stains. I tried not to think about it.

Maurice's Batman onesie was better than anything in the boxes, so he didn't bother taking anything, but while I was trying on stuff, he went over to speak to Grayson. After a brief discussion, Grayson opened a drawer in his desk and extracted a handful of spectacles, which Maurice tried until a pair seemed to work for him. They had thick black frames and some kind of wrapping on the middle bit where they were obviously broken.

Less than a day and Maurice had already levelled up from nerd to dork. If there was an uber-geek achievement to be won, he was well on his way to claiming it.

We retook our seats, looking like refugees from an Oxfam shop. Captain Grayson once again sat on the edge of his desk.

"Any more questions?"

No one said anything. Probably not because they didn't have questions, more likely because people had had enough. Nothing made sense, and the only question that really mattered had already been answered with a big fat no. We couldn't go home.

"My men are preparing food for you, but we weren't expecting so many, so it will take a little time. What I suggest you do is get into small groups of three or four and go have a look around town. It's a small place that was originally built to help visitors like yourself. The people are quite friendly, but bear in mind they all carry weapons, so be polite and don't start trouble. You might get a better idea of what to expect once you've seen a bit more. We'll ring a bell when the food's ready."

People slowly got up and started forming groups. I remained seated and moved my hands in front of me playing imaginary whack-a-mole, trying to feel for any kind of interaction. I couldn't shake the idea this had to be a game. If I could just access the status screen, maybe I'd be able to work out what I needed to do to level up.

"What are you doing?" asked Maurice.

"I'm looking for a way to access the user interface." I continued to pat the air.

"You really think this is a game?"

"Yep." I had no doubt, even though I had yet to find any actual evidence.

Maurice looked around, still squinting even though he had glasses now. "I don't think the technology exists for this level of immersion."

"I didn't think ogres existed either," I said.

"Fair point. Looks like everyone's leaving."

Having no luck with clicking on anything, I decided I should probably go have a look around town. The only people left in the room were a red-faced guy who had his arms folded and was staring at the ceiling for some reason, and two girls sat next to each other. One girl was a little plump with a round face that made her look fatter than she was. The other was very skinny and almost good-looking if it wasn't for her huge nose.

Quick sidebar: It may seem like I'm a sexist twat who only sees women in terms of their looks, but I don't think I treat women like they're inferior. I notice what I notice. I'm not going to pretend I'm some New Age moron who sees all life as part of the same beautiful tapestry. The first thing I noticed about Maurice was that he's black — and that's despite him wearing a Batman onesie. Does that make me racist? I think it means my eyes work. Feel free to judge me how you want.

I headed for the door and the girl with the big nose stood up.

"Don't you think we should form a group?" It came across as more accusation than question.

Damn, I'd almost made it to the door. I stopped and turned around. "Er, are you talking to me?"

"I get it, all right?" She seemed angry. At me in particular. "We're the ones nobody wants to hang out with. The losers. More reason we should stick together. Or are you just another bastard willing to leave two girls alone in this FUCKING SHITHOLE!"

The blast at the end had me leaning back. I don't really know how to handle angry girls, which is strange because my mother was like that for most of my childhood, so you'd think I'd be used to it.

Then again, maybe that's why it unnerves me so much. If you get angry back, they turn up the volume, no bass, all treble. If you try to speak gently, they get mad because you aren't taking them seriously. Back in the 1950s, you could slap a screaming woman and she'd thank you for calming her down. Try that these days and you might get a slightly different response.

"I don't know what you're so pissed at me for, I don't think you're a loser. If I don't seem sociable it's just because I find it difficult to talk to people, especially in big groups. I'm going to look around. If you want to come, nobody's stopping you."

I walked out the door with Maurice and the two girls falling in behind. Ceiling-staring guy got up and shuffled after us. Was this really my party? I had to ditch these losers as soon as possible.

5. Welcome to Probet

Outside, the road, more a dusty track, led in only one direction. Buildings ahead of us looked all the same. Wooden shacks of one storey. Noise and smells drifted towards us as we approached. It was hard to identify either.

"My name's Claire, by the way," said the girl with the big nose. "This is Flossie."

I turned to look at the plump red-head. "Really?"

"Oh ah, not really," she said in the broadest Brummie accent I'd ever heard. "Actually, it's Victoria, but everybody's always called me that since I were a babby."

"I'm Colin, and this is Maurice."

"Hello, ladies." Maurice smiled inanely.

I looked over to our fifth member, who was walking a few steps behind us with his hands behind his back and a tremendous interest in the sky. "What about you? Got a name?"

"Dudley Fenderson III." The voice that came out of his mouth was so posh, it sounded like the sort of voice you put on to mock posh people. He was tall, had a receding hairline even though he couldn't be more than nineteen or twenty, and no chin to speak of, so he definitely could be a member of the aristocracy. Or he had chosen this new stage to reinvent himself.

Introductions done, we turned a corner, and the main thoroughfare appeared in front of us. The whole town couldn't have been more than a dozen shacks. Various stores lined either side of the main street.

The first was a blacksmith's, a large open area with a roof over it and an intense fire burning in the middle. A variety of metalware hung on all sides. Weapons, armour pieces, pots and pans. A heavy-built man pounded away on an anvil with an enormous hammer.

"Go over and speak to him," I said to Maurice.

"About what?"

"I don't know, the price of stuff."

It turned out nobody wanted to talk to the blacksmith. Having a party made up of the socially awkward and chronically shy clearly had some drawbacks. In fact, it had nothing but drawbacks.

The idea of being unable to ask a question of someone in a shop, a person who's there to sell stuff, may seem ridiculous. But that means you've never experienced *the fear*. The inexplicable paralysis when you have to speak to someone official on the phone or attract the attention of a sales assistant in a shoe shop.

You could walk up to the nearest person and say, "Hey, I'd like to try this in a size nine, please," but you don't. You wait to be noticed, waving a shoe about, hoping someone offers to help.

If you have no idea what I'm talking about, congratulations, you're a well-adjusted member of society.

I steeled myself to do what had to be done, went over what I would ask in my head, and then walked purposefully towards the smithy. The others followed, but at a distance where they could pretend they had nothing to do with me.

"Excuse me? Hello?" Sweat ran down the back of my neck.

The blacksmith was completely bald, but with a huge walrus moustache. He wore a heavy leather apron that made him look like he had nothing on underneath. I desperately hoped that wasn't the case. He ignored me and continued to bang away — Pang! Pang! Pang! — red sparks flying in every direction. The hammer could have been borrowed from Thor. He picked a glowing object off the anvil with large pincers and plunged it in a bucket of water. Steam shot into the air.

"What is it?" he finally said without looking at me.

"How much for a dagger?" A number of daggers of varying sizes sat on a shelf.

"Depends." He started banging away again. Pang! Pang! Pang!

A bit rude, you might think. How did he expect to sell anything with that attitude? Well, you have to look at it from his perspective. A sweaty young man approaches holding up his trousers with one hand and carrying what looks like a table leg in the other. Are you thinking, '*Ho ho, big spender. I'll be able to shut up shop early tonight!*'? Of course not. More likely your first thought is, '*Shit, crazy homeless guy. Don't make eye contact, don't make eye contact.*'

"The cheapest one," I shouted over the noise. "How much?"

"Five bits," he shouted back, still not looking at me.

I thanked him and walked away. How much was five bits? No idea. I thought the currency would be coppers and silvers, maybe gold for expensive stuff. I had no idea if five bits would be easy to earn or not.

The others had overheard our conversation and were equally unsure.

"Hey, what weapons did you get?" I asked the others.

Claire pulled out a stick similar to mine. Dudley had two wooden balls attached by a string. Flossie looked sheepish, then put her hand down her top and took out a dagger.

"Bloody hell," said Maurice. "Nice."

I couldn't really tell if he meant the dagger or the cleavage it had emerged from. Both were quite impressive.

"Put it away," I said. "And don't show it to anyone." It was the sort of thing others might want for themselves. She quickly stuffed it back in its hiding place.

Clearly, we needed better weapons and this place would sell them to us. But first we had to make money. In an RPG, you killed monsters and they dropped loot. Money, potions, weapons. I looked at the stick in my hand and wondered if the local fast food joint was hiring.

6. Taking Stock

We wandered around a bit more. There was a place with animal skins hanging outside, like animal shaped rugs but with a strange yellow liquid dripping off them. The stink made me want to gag.

A man with oily black hair stood over a table set up outside the shop, cutting large skins with oversized scissors. Through the doorway I could see two girls carrying piles of skins from one place to another.

I guessed this guy turned skins into leather. Maybe he also turned them into clothing.

A sign leaning against the table had drawings of what looked like various animals — rabbits, pigs, dogs — with a number next to them. At least they used the same numbers as us, although the rest of their writing was gobbledegook to my eyes.

Either the numbers were the price you paid for each to type of material, or it was how much they paid you for bringing them skins you hunted. I considered the latter to be more likely, especially in a place like this that was basically a starter town.

In RPGs you always begin in a low level area where you make money by doing menial and repetitive tasks. Hunting low level animals for their skins seemed like an obvious way to make money and train your fighting skills at the same time. It was the sort of thing that provided an easy grind when playing on a computer. It probably wouldn't be so easy in real life. Assuming this was real life.

The lowest number on the board was for rabbit, with a one next to it. One bit? Five rabbits for a dagger, maybe? The most money was for a triangle. I had no idea what that represented, but it had the number fifty next to it.

The inhabitants of Probet milled around, chatting and greeting each other as you would expect. Maybe a dozen people shopped or went about their business, paying no attention to us. They were dressed plainly, like people from the Middle Ages or possibly frontier America. Animal skins, woollen garments, simple designs. Everyone wore trousers, no skirts for the ladies, no flowery blouses. Did everyone in this world dress like this, or were we just in the arse-end of nowhere and people scraped by best they could? Hard to say.

I looked closely to see if any of them were elves or dwarves or some other exotic species, but they all looked human, and not very attractive at that. No black or Asian people either. But not super white like Dudley, more Mediterranean, olive skin with Caucasian features.

Other stores sold clothing, household goods, animal feed, freshly butchered meat (exactly what kind of meat I couldn't say, but I swear one carcass had six legs). All basic stuff you might need for rural life.

I recognised some of the people checking out the different stores from our group. It looked like there were three other groups. The largest had six members, and was very clearly led by Golden Boy. He had no trouble walking up to shopkeepers and charming the socks off them.

Then there was an all female group of four, all very tall girls. The tallest had led the screaming complaints back at the hut. The other three looked like they had the permanent hump, a fixed pissed off expression stuck to their faces. Arms folded, head tilted, their eyes saying, "Yeah? What?"

I decided to give them a wide berth.

The last group of five was made up of what, if we were at school, I would refer to as the cool kids. Fancy haircuts, tattoos and even though they were wearing the same crappy clothes as us, they somehow managed to make it look stylish.

I'd put everyone in their late teens or early twenties. Probably university students. I left school at sixteen with the plan of getting a job and working my way up to some sort of senior position while kids my age wasted their time reading textbooks.

Brilliant sixteen-year-old me had come to the conclusion you didn't learn from reading, you learned from doing. Not so cocky nineteen-year-old me had been doing the same job for the last three years, watching college kids come in and zoom past.

We carried on peering through the doors of open stores, too nervous to go in and have a proper look. I knew I should have gritted my teeth and investigated everything, talked to everyone, but the thought of going up to one of these strangers from another world broke me out in a cold sweat. Nobody in my group took the initiative, they just hung behind me, waiting for something.

They did have fast food here, although they didn't appear to need more staff. At the far end of the street there were some food stalls manned by shifty-looking characters. Unfair of me since I didn't know them and had no reason to suspect them of anything, but if my cat went missing I wouldn't be surprised if a new meat dish suddenly appeared on the menu.

I stood in a daze, watching meats roasting on skewers and sugary pastries frying in oil. The smells were unfamiliar but still made my stomach churn with hunger.

So this was Probet, our home for the next few days at least. I had hoped for an obvious quest-giver who would send us off on a mission. Or maybe a gossip to provide us with useful intel. More and more it felt like we would have to actually start from scratch and survive using our own strengths and skills. Unfortunately, I had never used the gym membership I got last January, and although I had thought extensively about what to do in the event of a zombie apocalypse (haven't we all?), my plans mostly relied on being able to find a motorised chainsaw.

I had an uncomfortable sense of doom hanging over me. No way would we survive like this. We were the sort of party that needed to find an OP weapon and become legendary heroes by having a massively unfair advantage over everyone. As it was, no magic swords or glowing hammers had fallen into our hands, and there was an excellent chance we would all be killed by the first group of rabbits we stumbled across.

The clanging of a bell snapped me out of my trance. The others stood there, looking at me expectantly. If they wanted me to share some words of wisdom or deep insight, they'd be waiting a long time. I turned around and headed back.

7. Let's Eat

When we returned to the shed, we were shown through a side door into a courtyard. Captain Grayson handed each person a small tin box with a piece of flint inside. He demonstrated how to produce a spark by striking the side of the box.

Next, we each received a metal dish of cold stew and were pointed over to where four small fires, unlit, had been set up for us.

Suffice to say, we spent the next hour or so trying to start a fire while our stew slowly transformed into lumpy jelly. The tough part was getting the spark to catch, the larger pieces of wood adamantly refusing to have anything to do with flames of any kind. Luckily, we had all watched dozens of pseudo-documentaries where celebrities pretended to rough it in the wild.

We needed kindling of some kind, and Flossie solved the problem by pulling loose threads off her 'new' top and screwing them up into a bundle. Eventually we got the fire going, well after all the other groups had already started eating their hot stew.

The dishes had a small handle you used to hold it over the flames. The dish was metal. The handle was metal. I think you can guess the results.

We didn't have any utensils, so you had to wait for the stew to cool down before drinking it out of the edge of the dish. Made the whole point of heating it up rather pointless, but we were all so hungry we didn't care. It tasted bland and mainly consisted of potatoes (I think). Still, at least we now knew how to start a fire.

As we sat there, stew dribbling down our chins, I could hear the other groups chatting away, some of them laughing, others complaining. Our group sat in awkward silence. Until, that is, Maurice spoke up.

"I've been thinking. This is obviously a pretty backward kind of place, technologically speaking. If we could come up with an invention they haven't thought of yet, we could become bloody millionaires!"

"Sure," I said. "What did you have in mind?"

"Well, it can't be anything too advanced. It's not like we can suddenly make a computer or a helicopter or something like that. The technology isn't there. We need to come up with something low-fi. Something that a blacksmith could knock together, right?"

He looked around and the others nodded enthusiastically.

"I haven't really had time to think it through completely, but as a first suggestion, how about we invent the bicycle?"

I took the opportunity to introduce my own new concept to this world, the facepalm.

"You think what this society is crying out for is the bike?" I tried not to sound too dismissive. I'm not sure I succeeded, but it didn't seem to matter.

"Everything probably depends on horses at the moment, right?" continued Maurice, all fired up. "But horses cost money to look after. You've got to feed them, keep them in stables, they shit everywhere — it's a fulltime job. But a bike, you lean it against a wall, job done. These people will never have seen anything like it. They'll think we're wizards!"

Sadly, we'd probably all be dead long before he got his dream of recreating the Tour de France off the ground, although the idea of knights in full armour charging into battle on a ten-speed chopper had a certain appeal.

However, his idea did make me realise we should use our obvious advantage to good effect. The things we'd learned at school and seen on television about this sort of period in our own history should allow us to come up with something we could use — especially when it came to weapons.

Even stone age man figured out how to tie a rock to a stick and kill things with it, so we should be able to, too. As the others discussed exactly how pedals attached to gears, my mind drifted, thinking of simple weapons we could make. Bows and arrows would probably be quite fiddly to get right, plus you'd need a lot of arrows. And sharpened ends wouldn't be all that great compared to actual arrowheads.

After a bit of thinking the best idea seemed to be to make a sling. If it worked for David against Goliath, why not us? You needed a bit of string or something similar, and ammo was lying around everywhere. You just picked up small rocks off the ground. The more I thought about it, the better it seemed.

As I sat there feeling pleased with myself, I felt a presence next to me. I turned to find a girl standing there. It was her, the one with the freckled nose who had helped me back in the clearing. She didn't look very happy.

8. Room for One More?

"Hi, I'm Jenny." She said it to me, but quickly moved on to look at everyone else. "I was wondering if I could join your group."

The others awkwardly introduced themselves, at the end of which she turned back to me, obviously expecting me to do the same. I should make clear at this point, despite my general social ineptitude, there are two types of people I have no problems talking to. The first are those even more socially awkward than me (so, everyone sitting around the fire) and the other is pretty girls.

What? How can this be? Simple, really. I have absolutely no illusions about my chances, so there's no pressure to impress or come off cool.

I can only go by my own experiences, but I've always found that if a pretty girl talks to me it's because she wants something. If she flirts with me, it's something she definitely has no right to ask for, and she knows it.

I can't be bothered with people who are happy to use others like that. In fact, when it comes to pretty girls, I have a tendency to act like a dick.

"Why?" I asked her. She looked confused by the question. "You're with them, aren't you?" I pointed at Golden Boy's group. "Why would you want to leave them for us?"

She took a moment to think over her response. "All they talk about is killing stuff and how to get hold of better weapons. I'm not really comfortable with that stuff, so..." Her voice drifted off.

It made sense. Like the girl who made the outburst earlier, Jenny didn't fancy going on a killing spree either. But why choose us? I looked over at the other two groups.

The one nearest were the Cool Kids. Maybe even she felt intimidated by them, although I'm sure they'd accept her.

The other was the all girl group. If she really wanted to avoid killing anything, then that would seem the more obvious choice. But pretty girls often had issues with other girls. And having a few guys around to manipulate didn't hurt, either.

"I'm not sure why you think we're any different. Do you not remember the thing that attacked us? Killing is the only way we're going to survive here, and the people you're already with are probably going to be a lot better at it than us. If you can't do it yourself, you should stick with the people who can keep you safest, at least until something better comes along."

As soon as I said it, I realised it sounded like an insult. Like I was calling her an opportunist who took advantage of people until she could dump them for an upgrade. That's not how I meant it, but I also wouldn't deny that there was more than a small possibility she was one of those people.

Jenny seemed to have picked up on it as her face twisted from mild consternation into biting anger. "You're right. No point hanging with someone who has a panic attack every time he nearly gets stung by a bee."

I wanted to correct her, but what could I say? *"It wasn't a bee, it was a fairy"*? Not exactly a ringing endorsement for my masculinity, even though the fairy in question had looked more like Tinkerbell with rabies.

She turned around and walked away.

"Hey," I called after her. "Back in the clearing, thanks for helping me."

She paused and looked over her shoulder, confused. Rather than get into an argument, I had sincerely shown gratitude, just to mess with her. Classic dick move. She didn't say anything, just went back to her group who were all smiles at her return. I guess she hadn't told them she wanted out.

"Why did you do that?" asked Claire.

"What? I did her a favour. She's better off with them."

"Sure," said Claire. "You told her to piss off because you like her so m—"

I looked over to see why she had stopped in the middle of what she was saying, but she looked away, suddenly tending to the fire with great intensity.

It took me a moment to realise she must have come to the conclusion I really did send Jenny away because I liked her and wanted what was best for her. Maybe on a subconscious level that was true, but there was an even more pressing reason to send her packing.

Despite my claim that I don't see women as inferior, I also don't see them as equal to guys in all areas. That would be stupid. Clearly, the typical girl isn't as strong or aggressive as the typical boy. There are exceptions, of course, but I didn't think Jenny was going to turn out to have a love of MMA and a black belt in Brazilian jiu jitsu. In a world where we'd be fighting for our lives, the last thing our weak and feeble group needed was another girl.

9. Game Plan

"What I said about killing to survive is true. I know it's not what anyone of us wants to do, but pretending we can get through this by being decent, reasonable people isn't going to work."

They all looked at me like I was telling them they had to kill puppies and strangle kittens. Which I was.

"If we come up against anything like that ogre, we're dead. We can run away, but eventually we're going to have to fight, or starve to death. We have to learn how to kill. None of us is particularly strong or even sporty, which means we have to use a different approach."

"What approach?" said Claire. None of them seemed to have any idea what I was talking about.

"We have to be ruthless. And mean. Monsters aren't going to want to talk things over and find a compromise. There won't be any trade negotiations on Naboo."

Flossie raised her hand. "Ah don't know what you're talking about. What the fook is a Naboo?"

"You've never seen the Phantom Menace?" said Maurice. "I'm so jealous. Wish I could mindwipe that memory."

"Can we stay focused?" I didn't want a half-hour rant on the failings of George Lucas, and I could feel one about to erupt from Maurice. "What I'm saying is, back home people solved problems by asking the UN to apply sanctions. Here they hit things with sticks."

I waved my stick about for emphasis.

"Frankly, I don't know which is more useless, but at least with sticks you get a winner and a loser. If we don't want to be the losers, we need to fight. Do you see what I'm saying?"

They all nodded. They had no idea what I was saying.

"We're going to kill things. Some of them will be quite cute-looking. Weaker than us. Outnumbered and wanting to surrender. It doesn't matter. We can't afford to take prisoners or give them the benefit of the doubt. If they put their hands up, stab them in the face. If they wave a white flag, stab them in the face and use the flag as a scarf. We can't hesitate or take risks or waste anything. Nobody is going to help us, and everyone is going to try to fuck us over."

"You don't know that for sure," said Claire.

"Look at us. Why would anyone think we'd be anything but a pushover? That's our only advantage, that they'll underestimate us and give us the chance to strike first. And when we do, we have to go all in. No doubting halfway through. If you agree on a plan you have to commit to it, no matter how shitty it makes you feel. Afterwards, you can refuse to do it again, or make changes or whatever, but in the middle of a fight you have to do your part or you'll just get the rest of us killed."

They seemed to be sort of getting it now, but at the same time, they also seemed less keen on the whole 'kill everything' murder-frenzy I was advocating.

"I know it won't be easy, and nobody has to do anything they don't want to. You can go off on your own if you want. Or all together and leave me on my own. But it won't be any easier. You'll still have to kill stuff one way or another. Try to think of it as a game. You've all played video games, right?"

Flossie raised her hand again. "You mean like Candy Croosh."

"No, not really. More like..." I tried to think of a more appropriate phone app. "Clash of Clans? You know it? You fight people weaker than you, take their stuff, build up your strength. We have to do that."

"But this isn't a game, is it?" said Claire.

It was hard to say. I still felt like everything was too much like an RPG for it not to be a game, but I still hadn't found any proof.

Claire started poking the fire again. "We might even have to kill other people, that's what you're saying, aren't you?"

"Ooh," said Flossie, getting animated. "It's like *The Hoonger Games*!"

"Yes," I said. "A bit like that."

"I fookin' love Katniss."

"Those films were terrible," Maurice insisted vigorously. "Absolutely shocking."

A 'book versus movie' debate broke out.

I looked over at Jenny sitting quietly while the rest of her group chatted away, and a thought popped into my head. Who would die first, me or her? I turned my attention back to my group as they discussed the finer points of Peeta versus Gale, and the answer to my morbid question stared me in the face.

I got to my feet and said, "Bathroom," by way of explanation to the inquiring faces looking up at me. "The thing about *The Hunger Games*, though, still a better love story than *Twilight*, right?" I dropped that literary hand grenade and walked away.

The truth was I didn't need to use the loo — quite possibly I'd never have to ever again if the feeling of my intestines solidifying was anything to go by — I just wanted to get out of there and be on my own for a bit.

I walked through the shed, out the other side and made my way back to the main street. It was hard to tell the exact time, but I'd guess around lunchtime, maybe a bit later.

The sun was high and exceptionally warm. I felt relieved not to have anyone with me, just a stick in one

hand and the waist of my trousers in the other to stop
them falling down.

10. Walk on the Wild Side

The blacksmith wasn't in front of his place banging away. The forge still burned fiercely but nobody seemed to be about, or so I thought until I saw a young guy sitting on a stool near the back, dozing. I really wanted to have a proper look around the place, but the guy looked pretty beefy, and I didn't fancy getting caught snooping.

I moved on to the leather store a little further along. This place also seemed deserted. Maybe everyone was off having lunch, or possibly they had a siesta type culture like Spanish people, afternoon nap and then back to work in the evening when things cooled down. Either way it was very quiet, although I suspected the girls who had been working in the back were probably still around.

What I was interested in didn't need me to go inside. I casually walked closer, scanning the floor for any off-cuts or strips of discarded leather. There were actually quite a lot of them. I took a brief look around, dropped to one knee like I was tying my laces (hard to do on boots without any) and quickly grabbed everything I could off the dusty ground.

My haul consisted of around a dozen leather strips of varying lengths, and a bunch of scraps. I got to my feet and speed-walked away to the other side of the street, desperately hoping not to hear someone shout, "Stop! Thief!"

The first thing I did was to use the longest piece as a belt for my baggy trousers. My hands shook so much from my little heist, it took a number of goes to tie a knot. I slipped my stick inside the belt like a wooden sword hanging at my waist. Once I got that sorted, I waited for my heart to stop hammering and then checked the rest of the pieces.

They were strong and supple, if a little hairy. I was sure I could make some sort of sling, maybe a couple. The larger pieces might even be enough to make a sap. From what I could remember from a YouTube video I had came across during my wasted youth, all you needed was some lead encased in leather with a strap to give it some whip. By all accounts, a ridiculously effective weapon for breaking bones and knocking people out.

I looked across the street at the smithy, wondering what I might find discarded over there. Before I knew what I was doing, I had wandered closer, my eyes glued to the floor. Old nails, broken handles, rusty keys — it was like a treasure trove of scrap metal. Surely nobody would mind if I took one or two bits of junk?

My hand was on the verge of reaching down when a clatter made me look up. The guy dozing on the stool was now standing and holding a knife. He looked terrified.

I whipped my head around to see what was freaking him out, but there was no one there. Slowly it dawned on me the thing scaring him was me.

I raised my hands. "Hi. I was just looking around."

"I know what you are," he said in a shaky voice. "You people come here, take what you want, kill for fun." His voice gradually got higher-pitched until it squeaked. "Just leave." The knife trembled in his hand.

"Er... I don't kill for fun. I've never killed anything, not even the stuff I eat."

He looked confused.

"Where I come from, violence is considered a crime. People get locked up for hitting each other."

His confusion turned into disbelief. "You lie. Your kind loves blood and death. You-you-you love it!"

He looked about my age, maybe a little older. He could easily take me in a fight, for sure. His arms were all puffed up with muscles. And no, I'm not gay, so stop thinking it.

He was probably the blacksmith's son or his apprentice (maybe both), which gave me an idea.

"Listen, I don't want to be here. I don't know how to fight and I don't want to kill anything, but I don't want to be eaten by monsters either. Nobody's explained anything to us, and I can't even read or write your language. That sign over there." I pointed at the board in front of the leather place. "Those pictures of animals with numbers next to them, does that mean if I bring dead animals, the guy over there will give me money for them?"

He nodded. "The tanner will pay you for skins."

"One bit for a rabbit?"

A smile broke out on his face. The kind of smile reserved for when you hear something really stupid. "One bit? No, one chob."

"What's a chob? Is it less than a bit?"

"Ten chobs, one bit."

Damn. That meant a five bit dagger would take fifty rabbit skins. Were there even that many rabbits in this place? Still, that meant only ten pig skins or five dogs. That didn't seem so bad, assuming they were the kinds of pigs and dogs we had back home.

"What about the triangle for fifty chobs. What animal is that?"

"Any beast."

"Rabbit, pigs and dogs aren't beasts?"

He shook his head. "They're vermin. They ruin crops and worry cattle."

"So beasts are..."

"Wolves, bears, elk..."

Right. Stuff that could actually kill you.

He still had his knife out, but not in such a threatening manner as before.

"The only weapon I have is this." I showed him my

stick. "So I don't think you need to be scared of me."

"I'm not scared!" he squeaked.

"I don't have any money, so I can't afford to buy anything yet. But when I do get some money, do you think I could buy stuff directly from you?"

The question seemed to confuse him. "What do you mean?"

"The stuff the blacksmith makes is good, but it's expensive. You're his assistant, right? I thought if I buy the weapons you make, it might be cheaper."

He lowered the knife and shook his head. "I do not have a hammer. You can't forge iron without a hammer."

"Can't you use the blacksmith's?"

He looked at me like I'd suggested he use a dead baby to make a hat. "A blacksmith's hammer cannot be touched without his permission. Master trains me once a day in the use of the hammer, if he's in a good mood. I only make what he allows."

Sounded like a bullshit system to me, but I was getting good information out of this guy and didn't want it to stop.

"So how do you get your own hammer. You have to pass a test or something?"

"There are only two ways." He sounded quite bitter, maybe even sorry for himself. "Either you inherit your master's when he passes on, or a weapon you created is used to kill a superior beast."

"A superior beast?"

"One that is able to speak."

"You mean like people?"

His eyed me suspiciously. "People are not beasts."

"No, of course not, I just meant..." I don't know what I meant so I changed the subject. "Wait, if you need a hammer to make a weapon, but you need a weapon to kill a superior beast in order to get a hammer... how does that work?"

The bitter look returned to his face. "It's not meant to be easy. Otherwise there would be too many smithies and not enough work to go around."

I started to understand. It was clearly in a blacksmith's interest not to let his apprentice get too good, too quick. If the guy you trained sets up shop nearby, you're going to end up losing business to him.

"Look, I don't know if I'm ever going to be any good at monster hunting. Probably, I'll be one of the first to get myself killed. But if you make me a simple weapon, something that doesn't require a hammer to make, I'll use it. And if I manage to kill a superior beast, I'll come back and you'll be able to claim your hammer."

My suggestion took him aback. "Why would you do that for me?"

"Because you'll owe me, and sell me weapons for half-price for the rest of your life."

He grinned. Finally, I was speaking a language he understood.

11. Not Excalibur

The blacksmith's apprentice folded his arms. "Making a weapon without a hammer won't be easy. What sort of thing were you thinking?" He raised his hand and rubbed his chin with a calloused thumb.

The truth was I wasn't thinking of anything. I had come up with the idea he could make me a weapon just so I could get something for free. I certainly had no plans to go looking for a superior beast. I had visions of talking gorillas hunting me down on horseback with nets.

"Erm, well, what about something with a sharp point? If I could stab it in the eye or the ear I might get lucky and kill it in one shot."

He nodded. Apparently he knew what I meant, even though I was making it up on the spot. He moved over to a box on a table and clinked and clanked through it until he found a metal rod. It looked pretty old and worn, roughly the length of my forearm. A railing from a garden gate or something like that.

Over the next half hour he heated up the middle of the rod in the forge, pulling and twisting either end so the glowing red part got thinner and thinner until it finally split into two. He doused both end in the bucket of water and now had two shorter rods with pointed ends.

He inspected them both and selected the one with the more pronounced point. Then he heated up the other end, bent and curved it as it became more malleable, until he curved it right over so it looked like a cup handle.

He did this using large pliers. He didn't have any gloves on or goggles and ignored sparks that splashed onto his bare arms. Health and safety would have had a field day.

Once he had cooled it all down in the all-purpose

bucket of water, he took it over to a large grinding stone set up like a spinning wheel with a pedal to get it up to high speeds.

It occurred to me that if they had invented the pedal and wheel already, chances were someone had also come up with the bicycle. Maurice would be devastated.

Bright, white sparks flew in all directions as he ground the end of the rod to an even sharper point.

When he'd finished, he handed over what was basically a spike with a handle. He hesitated momentarily, but then let me have it.

"It's made of scrap, so it won't be missed."

I turned it over in my hand. It was certainly better than my stick. I pricked my finger with the point and a drop of blood bubbled up immediately.

"By the way," I said, deciding to press my luck, "do you have any more scrap I could have?"

"Like what?"

"Old nails, lumps of lead, wire, anything like that? Doesn't have to be in good condition."

He didn't look too keen on giving me any more handouts.

"What about the stuff on the floor?" I pointed to a rusty iron nail wedged between the floorboards.

He grimaced at the idea of me wanting trash, but shrugged and said, "Help yourself."

I got on my knees and quickly grabbed every little thing I could find before he changed his mind or his boss turned up. I pulled up the bottom of my shirt and put everything I found in the fold. Once I had picked the floor clean I stood up and thanked him.

"You are a strange man," he said. I couldn't help but feel pleased he saw me as a man, strange or otherwise. "What is your name?"

"Colin."

"Co-leen. Even your name is strange. I'm Kizwat—" yeah, I had the strange name "—if you do manage to kill a superior beast, I will keep my part of the deal."

I nodded. The chances of me killing a regular beast seemed very low, so a superior beast probably wasn't even a possibility. Still, if I did manage it somehow, I would definitely come back and get this guy his hammer. My own personal blacksmith would be pretty cool.

"One more thing," I said. "Where would I find rabbits to hunt?"

"If you go east out of town, beyond the wheatfields there are wild meadows. There should be plenty there."

"Okay, thanks. And, which way is east?"

He pointed over my head. I could see him regretting his decision to help me already. Having got him to the point where he was actually getting annoyed with me, I decided not to push my luck any further and left.

Instead of heading back to the shed, I snuck down the side of the smithy and over a fence into a small piece of scrub land. I dumped the content of my shirt on the ground and inspected my acquisitions.

There were six nails, each at least the length of my finger, half of them crooked and all of them rusty. I did a little foraging and found a fist-sized rock which I used to pound the nails through one end of my stick. I took as much care as I could not to splinter the wood but the nails still had sharp points and went through surprisingly easily.

The result was a fearsome weapon, with vicious-looking barbs. If the nails didn't kill you, tetanus probably would.

Excited by how well I was doing, I moved on to the leather scraps. I took a square about the size of a large stamp and poked holes in either side using the spike I'd got off Kizwat. I tied a long strip to each hole. It made a little hammock. I grabbed a handful of small stones off the ground and placed one in the cradle.

Spinning it around worked well. Getting it to release proved a bit trickier. My first attempt stayed firmly in the cradle and smacked me on the top of my head. Painful. A few goes later, I got it to fly out at considerable speed. In the wrong direction, but still, it would be an effective weapon once I got the hang of it.

I estimated I had enough material to make three more. It was so straightforward, I could probably make another couple using the rags left over in the clothes box back at the shed.

The other bits of metal didn't seem to have an obvious use right now, but I wrapped them up as best I could and headed back. With my rusty nail club and my sling of infinite ammo, I felt ready to strike fear in the hearts of rabbits everywhere.

12. Lock and Load

Just before I walked through the shed door, I had a sudden urge to make a sharp 180 and go off on my own. Whenever I played an MMO on my computer, I chose to play solo. Online games are designed to be a social activity. You can speak to people as you play, plan out and coordinate your attacks, chat about this and that. You share the highs and lows, the laughter and the tears.

Not me. I liked to explore alone and try to deal with monsters on my own. It took longer, but it was just a lot less stressful that way. Of course, I would occasionally join a group to do a dungeon or a raid, but more often than not you'd run into a bunch of arseholes.

People who took the game too seriously, swore and screamed at anyone who made a mistake or didn't already know the mob attack patterns, and generally used the game as their personal venting platform. And then there was the whining when it came to rolling for loot...

Playing solo meant you could do what you want, make as many mistakes as it took, and generally enjoy yourself without relying on anyone or having anyone rely on you. Much more fun.

But I wasn't here to have fun. On my PC, if things got hairy, I could try again or logout. Or even complain to the GM and get them to rollback my character. In this world, there was a good chance game over really meant game over. If I wanted to survive, I'd need help. People watching my back, ready to offer me a helping hand when I came up short.

I wasn't too sure if the idiots I was stuck with would turn out to be those people, but I didn't think being on my own would have many advantages right now.

I walked through the empty shed and out into the courtyard. The other groups had left. Where they'd gone, I had no idea. My group sat around our now smouldering fire. Maurice cleaned his glasses with the sleeve of his onesie. Dudley hugged his knees while rocking back and forth like a disturbed child. Flossie had a fixed smile on her face, the kind nervous people have when they don't want others to think they're feeling nervous. And Claire scowled as she poked the remnants of the fire with her stick.

Perhaps going solo needed some serious reconsideration?

"You're back," said Claire, sounding angry. "I thought you'd gone off and left us."

"Must have been a hell of a dump," said Maurice. "You took ages."

I ignored them both and dropped my recently acquired items on the ground. Leather scraps, metal junk and some pebbles. I expected them to look at me like a nutter who had brought them trash, but they all stared wide-eyed with amazement.

"What did you do to that?" Maurice pointed at the stick resting on my shoulder. I lowered it to the ground, spiky end down, obviously. The rusty nails looked nasty.

"Upgrade. Should scare off a few critters. Probably do myself an injury if I try to actually use it in a fight. Flossie, lend me that knife a minute."

She didn't hesitate for a second, just took out the dagger and handed it over. How was I ever going to turn this bunch into the cynical, jaded bastards they needed to be to survive?

I used the knife to cut off a piece of leather and gave it to Maurice.

"Use this to fix your shoe."

He had a broken clasp on his left sandal. He quickly

tied it together making the shoe ten times more secure.

"Thanks, man. Really." He grinned at me. Amazing how the little things make you feel when you have sod all.

"Okay, I want to show you something."

I picked up my sling and a small stone. I loaded the sling and spun it around my head. I had managed to make it work earlier, but with everyone watching, my heart crawled into my throat and the sweat in my palms threatened to let the sling slip out of my grip. If I screwed this up I'd look a right fool.

Fortunately, when I whipped the sling to release the stone, it flew out in the right direction. It went up at a forty-five degree angle, so only a good shot if we ever went giraffe hunting, but still good enough to demonstrate the weapon's use.

The others burst into spontaneous applause.

"Marvellous. Absolutely marvellous," said Dudley. I think they were his first words since introducing himself.

Their impressed expressions only embarrassed me more. "Er, yeah, anyway, obviously it'll take practice to get good, but with something like this you can hit the target from far away. A lot safer than hand to hand fighting."

Using Flossie's knife, I cut up the other strips of leather and made some more slings. Together with some rags from the box of clothes in the shed, I was able to make one for everybody. They stood there, each admiring their new toy. They didn't see them as tools of death, but they would.

"Right," I said. "I reckon we've got quite a bit of daylight left. Let's go hunting."

13. A Hunting We Will Go

We left the shed and headed east. Everyone was very impressed I knew which direction east was, but I told them how I found out, quickly lowering their expectations.

I could have let them believe I had an innate ability to know where I was going, but then they might have started relying on me to tell them what to do. Some people like that sort of thing — being looked up to, asked their opinion, admired. Best way to make yourself look an idiot, in my experience.

We quickly came to the fields of wheat Kizwat had mentioned, ringed by a wooden fence. On the way into town, Grayson had made it clear fields were to be walked around, not through. Apparently, only in movies is it considered acceptable to run through a field trampling all the crops.

It meant it would take us longer to get to the other side, but we needed the time to get used to the slings.

The person who had most problems was Flossie. She would get it whizzing around her head and then be unable to get it to stop. She would try to fling the stone out, but after failing a couple of times and nearly 'lamping' herself (as she put it), she would start squealing and try to run away from the strap whirling overhead, even though it was attached to her hand.

Or she would release the whole thing, sending the sling flying off into the distance. And then we'd spend ten minutes looking for it in the undergrowth.

Everyone else soon got the hang of getting the pebbles to shoot out, if not the ability to control where they went. It didn't matter where you stood, you were in the firing line. In fact the safest place seemed to be directly in front of the person shooting.

Still, the little stones did ricochet off the fence posts with enough force to suggest they'd do some serious damage if they ever hit flesh and blood.

We weren't very good, but the challenge of learning a new skill was quite entertaining. Even Flossie eagerly tried again after each failed attempt. The only person who didn't appear to be enjoying the training session was Claire. She wasn't that bad, managing to get the sling to work most of the time — although she did smack herself in the leg occasionally (as we all did) — but her face indicated she really didn't want to be doing this. Or possibly it was the thought of what we planned to do with our new skill.

"You know," I said, "even if you don't want to kill any animals, you should still learn how to use that thing properly. For self-defence."

The others were all spread out. We needed to keep a decent distance between us to avoid smacking each other on the arms with wayward spinning (something we learned the hard way). Claire had taken to strolling along, whipping her empty sling against her palm.

"Why?" she said, like a surly teenager. "What good will it do against an ogre?"

"It isn't just monsters and beasts you have to watch out for. This is a primitive society, and you're a girl. I don't know what it's like for women here, but I'm pretty sure there are men who treat them like crap and force them to do things they don't want to do."

Somehow I found myself talking about something I wasn't very comfortable with, and trying my best to avoid using certain words.

"Yeah, well I doubt I'll have to worry about that."

I stopped and looked at her. She stopped and looked

right back at me. She had a thin face, but very clear skin. Her eyes were a pale grey, which was unusual, and her hair was straight and long, a mixture of brown and dark blonde streaks. The nose, of course, was unmissable. Not crooked, just large with flared out nostrils. She wasn't pretty, but she wasn't a gargoyle either.

"Are you fishing for a compliment?" I asked her.

"No. What are you talking about?"

We had entered some kind of race to see who could sound more annoyed.

"You'd be happier if men considered you worth raping, would you?" She'd made me use that word, which annoyed me even more. "Because unless you have a detachable vagina and you left it back home, it's as likely to happen to you as anyone else."

"Fuck you. That's not what I'm saying." We were about even on the annoy-o-meter. "I don't even know why you're bringing this up. It's horrible. Not all guys are like that."

"No, not all guys. But enough of them so that you should be careful and learn to take care of yourself. You can't rely on us to come save you if some evil bastard drags you into the bushes. This is like a third world country. Not the ones where you go on holiday and get beautiful silk scarves for super cheap. I mean the ones where they have child soldiers and genocides and drug cartels running towns. And you know what all those sorts of places have in common? They treat their women like shit."

The others had started to walk towards us, probably thinking we'd stopped to have some kind of meeting.

"What are you talking about?" Claire raged. "How is this place like that?" She opened her arms wide indicating the world around us; the golden wheat swaying in the breeze, the forest trees in the distance dappled with sunlight, the fluffy clouds innocently floating by. It certainly didn't seem to be a place full of horror and despair. "You don't know anything. You're just trying to scare me so I'll do what you say, learn to hit things with this stupid contraption."

She spun the sling around her finger, first one way then the other.

"Claire," I retorted with no intention of backing down, although I really have no idea why it had become such a big deal to me, "this is a world where you have to kill to survive. It's not much of a leap from using violence to get the things you need, to using violence to get the things you want. And for a lot of men, one of those 'things' is women. Why not? What's anyone going to do about it? Call the police?"

The other three were now standing around us, looking a bit miffed by the conversation they'd walked into.

"So you're saying I should watch out for all guys, including the three of you? Once you get used to using violence to kill small animals, you might decide to use it to get some action in the bedroom?" She wiggled her hips suggestively, playing up to the audience, her face twisted with sarcasm.

"Maybe," I said calmly, refusing to rise to her baiting. "I don't think any of us three is the type, but who knows? Same with the rest of the guys that came here with us. Any of them could turn out to be a massive douchebag."

"And yet you sent that girl back to the biggest douchebags of all."

She was talking about Jenny, and I was sort of pleased she thought of Golden Boy and his cronies as douchebags, but she had a point. If Jenny liked one of those guys and hooked up with him, it would probably keep her safe. But if she rejected them, things might get iffy. At best she might get thrown out of the group. At worse... I really didn't want to think about it.

Flossie took my pause for thought as an opportunity to step in. She jumped in front of Claire with her arms spread out, like a referee stopping a boxing match.

"Alright, that's enough. We got things to do, can't be chatting all day. Ah get what you're saying, Colin. We just got to be careful. Even back home, there's some places you don't go at night by yourself. Same thing, right? Right, Claire?"

"Sure," said Claire. "Whatever." She turned to Maurice and Dudley, both of whom looked terrified by the thought they might be asked to share their thoughts on the matter. "I just want you two to know I don't think you'd do anything like that. I think you're both really great guys." Then she turned back to me. "You, I'm not so sure about."

Even though she was just being spiteful and didn't really mean it (I hope), it still stung to hear her say that. She flinched a little. I think she could see she had hurt me and perhaps she thought she had gone too far. Or maybe I was imagining it.

"Don't worry," I said, rather more viciously than I intended. "I won't lay a finger on you. Ever."

The flash of pain in her eyes told me I had scored a direct hit, and I immediately regretted what I said, or at least the way I had put it.

"In any case," I continued, trying to dig my way out of the hole I'd jumped into, "I'm pretty sure the only way I'll get laid in this place is if one of those douchebags sticks me on their dick and uses me as a condom."

There was a moment of silence and then Maurice burst out laughing, followed by the others, including Claire. I'm not sure it was that funny a joke, but the tension needed to be broken, and apparently the idea of me being sexually assaulted was something everyone could have a good laugh about.

14. Kill the Wabbit

We finally worked our way around the wheatfield and reached the other side. A fallow green field on a gentle slope led to the top of a low hill, beyond which there was a huge open area of grass, completely flat and disappearing into the distance in all directions.

The country was called Flatland, and I guessed this was why.

And everywhere you looked there were rabbits. Hundreds of them.

They didn't look exactly like the rabbits back home. They were about the same size — brown, black and a few white ones — with long, floppy ears, but they had elongated faces, and instead of a pom-pom tuft, a pinkish stub for a tail. They didn't hop, either. More scurried about.

"Aw!" said Flossie. She walked up to the nearest one and picked it up.

She picked it up! I was stunned. If it was going to be this easy we'd have five daggers each by sundown.

Of course, it was not going to be that easy.

The rabbit turned its fluffy face to look at Flossie and then snarled at her, revealing not a cute Bugs Bunny overbite, but dozens of triangular fangs. I swear I heard the theme from *Jaws* start to play.

Flossie screamed and threw the rabbit. She didn't just drop it, she launched it. It flew through the air, the first of its kind to go airborne, I'd be willing to bet. It landed on the grass with a 'flump' sound, rolled a couple of times, shook its head and scurried off.

After that, the other rabbits were wary of us, and every time we took a step towards one, it took a step further away. No matter, we had come prepared with weapons, and we had picked up plenty of pebbles on the way. The time had come to see if we had what it took to defeat the rabbits of Flatland.

Short answer: no.

We quickly realised a few things. First, we had to spread out. A couple of near-misses (not the rabbits, each other) made it clear we were more of a danger to ourselves than to the rabbits. It also helped if we were sort of opposite each other so if one person's shots drove the rabbits away, it would be towards someone else. Although, directly opposite wasn't a good idea either.

What became readily apparent was that aiming at a living thing was very different to aiming at a wooden post. Not just because they moved — the rabbits sort of ambled about but mainly stayed in the same place unless we got too close — but because the idea of snuffing out their existence made your heart hammer in your chest and sweat break out all over your body.

Still, we all gave it a go, sending stones whizzing across the meadow, hitting nothing but air and turf. All except for Claire. She just stood there with one arm hanging down, the other hand holding onto her elbow. I don't think she was refusing to try, I think it was more that she was paralysed by indecision and couldn't bring herself to get on with it, even though she was probably telling herself to do just that.

She looked miserable. And it was pissing me off.

"What?" She had caught me staring at her. "What do you want me to do?"

"Nothing," I said. "What I said back in town, about nobody having to do anything they don't want to, I meant it. This isn't a democracy, you don't have to follow the majority vote. Nobody's going to bully you to go along. If you agree to do something, do it. If you don't, don't."

"And that's fine, is it?" she said, angry as ever.

"If you're happy with being a burden on others, then yes." I nodded towards the others as they groaned and yelled at every near and not so near miss. "They won't turn their backs on you or kick you out."

Her eyes narrowed. "And what about you?"

"Same as you don't have to do anything you don't want to, neither do I. If I don't think it's worth staying with you guys, I'll leave. I don't want to waste my days arguing over every little thing and carrying people who don't even want to try."

Claire's mouth shrunk into her face. Her body trembled, and I thought she might start crying. But she lowered herself to her knees and picked out some stones from the grass. She stood up again and loaded her sling, spun it and then whipped it down. Before the stone had even landed, she had reloaded and fired off another one. Then another, and another.

She wasn't aiming — most of the time she was staring at me — but they came out fast and low, peppering the ground around the rabbits, sending them scurrying off.

When her hand was empty, she got down on her knees again and collected more stones. She got up and started firing again. Tears streaked down her face, but she kept at it, getting faster and faster.

Did I feel like a shit? Yes. Was I going to tell her to stop, that it was okay, she didn't have to do it? No. If blackmail was the way to get her head in the game, so be it.

And then she hit one. Right in the side. It seemed to jump sideways and then fell over.

Claire dropped her sling and put both hands over her mouth, horrified. The others saw and cheered, thinking she'd be as delighted as them. I walked over to the body of the victim. It had brown fur apart from a black hole where the stone had hit it. As I reached down, it suddenly got back up, shook its whole body, and scampered away.

There wasn't any blood. It wasn't a wound, just a bruise. Claire's gasp turned into sobbing and Flossie rushed over to console her, probably thinking she was upset to have failed, whereas it was probably more likely relief. But she had pushed herself to do what she knew had to be done, and after she recovered from the shock of hitting something, she was able to try again.

She would occasionally look over at me as she sent her shots across the meadow, but the expression was not so much resentment at what I was forcing her to do, as it was determination to prove me wrong. That she didn't need to be carried, by me or the others.

It took a couple more hours before we finally bagged our first rabbit. The person who got it was, of course, Flossie. Still by far the worst of us, she managed to hit it right in the eye. A shot I'm a hundred percent certain she would never be able to make again. Why? Because the rabbit she had aimed at was a fat, black one about five metres in front of her. The one she hit was about twenty metres directly behind her.

I decided we should call it a day after that. The sun was fairly low in the sky, but we had plenty of light. More of an issue was that we hadn't brought any water with us, and it had been a warm afternoon. The others were happy to head back.

Dudley picked up our prize and held it up by its hind legs while the others tentatively took a closer look. Even Claire had come to accept this as something we had to get used to.

As we set off, I looked over my shoulder at the sun falling towards the horizon and got a strange prickly feeling on the back of my neck. It took me a few moments to understand the cause of it. The sun was setting in the east.

15. May I Take Your Coat?

As soon as we got back to Probet, we headed for the tanner's store, proudly carrying our one rabbit like it was a great accomplishment. Which it was for us, so not surprisingly we felt a little pleased with ourselves.

The tanner soon brought us back to earth.

"We don't take the whole thing, just the skin." He was outside his shop, slicing up a stiff looking piece of leather that had come from some huge animal.

"How do we skin it?" Maurice asked. The fact someone spoke other than me was an indication of how far we'd come. At this rate, we'd hit normal in a couple of months.

The tanner paused long enough to give us a disparaging look, then continued with cutting the leather with an incredibly sharp pair of shears.

"If you show us how to skin this one," I said, "you can have the skin for free." It seemed a fair trade. We wouldn't get any money (although I'm not sure we'd be able to buy a whole lot with one chob), but we'd have learned a new skill, and that was much more important in an RPG. Yes, I still felt this was a game.

The tanner, like merchants everywhere, was hardwired to never turn down a good deal. He leaned back and called out. "Miri, come here a moment."

One of the girls from the back of the shop came running out. She was small and looked to be in her early teens. Her brown hair was tied back in a simple ponytail, revealing a serious face. His daughter, his assistant, his wife — hard to say. Maybe all three.

"Miri, show these visitors how to skin a rabbit."

A glimmer of irritation passed across the girl's face, but she nodded. She wiped her hands on the front of her pinny and snatched the rabbit from Dudley. She stomped around the side of the shop without saying anything.

We followed her to the back where large wooden tubs of foul smelling liquid bubbled and steamed. The other girl had a long pole in her hands and was using it to stir the contents of each tub.

Miri kneeled down on a patch of dirt and lay the rabbit down. She took a knife out of the front pocket of the pinny.

With two deft slices she cut the rabbit across the middle and from neck to crotch. Then she peeled back the skin and pulled it off like she was taking a baby out of a babygrow. A dead baby out of babygrow stuck to its skin, only much more gut-churning.

Her movements were sharp and forceful, but the skin came away in one piece, only the loud tearing sound indicated it was actually attached to the rabbit.

We all watched open-mouthed. It was disgusting and impressive at the same time. She did it so smoothly and quickly it looked easy, but I expected we'd find it anything but when we tried to do it ourselves.

She threw the skin into one of the tubs and handed me the pink carcass. It was hard not to think of it as something out of a horror movie. *Bunny Hunter.* "This killer doesn't just take your life, he takes your skin!" But that was just my soft middle-class sensibilities. This was food. At least, I hoped it was.

I took it from her, forcing myself not to react to the revulsion welling up inside me as I felt slippery smoothness of the flesh in my hand. "Can we eat this?"

She made a face that could have been disapproval, or just annoyance that we were taking up so much of her time. To be honest, with its long snout and pink tail, the rabbit looked more like a large, long-eared rat. It's not surprising there'd be a similarity, since rabbits are rodents, but still, not the most appetising thought.

"If you want. You have to gut and clean it first."

"And how do we do that?"

She gave me the same look Kizwat had when I asked him which way was east. But she took the rabbit back and put it on the ground. She stabbed it in the chest and dragged her knife through the body. Then she pulled the incision apart, cracking bones as she opened it up to reveal the innards. *Bunny Hunter 2*. "This time he wants what's inside!"

She flipped it over and everything fell out in a big red mess. She used her knife to scoop out the last of it, slicing off the attached parts. The smell of blood and shit cut through the already acrid air.

Miri handed me the rabbit. "Wash it properly. Anything else?" She said it in a tone that suggested the answer should be, "No."

"No," I said. "Thank you."

We all felt a bit queasy after seeing the rabbit peeled and gutted like that, but I assumed we would eventually get used to it. We left her to her work and set off back to the shed. We still hadn't made any money, but we had dinner sorted.

16. A Gift From Prometheus

It was evening, and the light had started to fade by the time we returned to the shed. Captain Grayson was sitting on the edge of his desk with a stack of grey blankets next to him.

"Welcome back," he said. "I see you've been..." His voiced trailed off as he saw the rabbit and he pulled a strange face I couldn't quite place. "Here, you'll need these. It gets a little chilly at night."

He handed each of us a blanket. They weren't very big — more shawl than cloak — made of a scratchy, wiry material. We happily took them from him.

"Do you have anything we can use to carry water?" I asked him.

He raised an eyebrow at me and then jumped off the desk. He walked over to a wall that had a large cloth hanging over it, which turned out to be curtains. He parted them enough to reach in and pulled out another box. This one had a bunch of water skins in it.

I felt a bit irked that he hadn't told us about them before, but it seemed like it was kind of a test to only give us certain things when we asked for them. It made me realise we should have been asking a lot more questions. I tried to think of what else we might need and came up with a complete blank.

There were a couple of soldiers waiting by the exit to the courtyard with a bucket of stew. They slopped out a ladleful into a metal dish and handed it to us as we walked out. It looked like the same stuff we had for lunch, but at least we could add some rabbit to it now.

Two of the other groups had already returned and set up for the night. On the right, the Cool Kids had a decent-sized fire going, and they had what looked like chickens roasting on a spit.

On the left side, Golden Boy and company had gone one better. They had a whole pig over a roaring inferno. Their fire was huge, and the pig, some kind of boar judging by the tusks, was already a golden brown.

Members of both groups had water skins at their feet or hanging from belts, most of them bigger and in better condition than the ones we got. Apparently they were a lot quicker on the uptake than us.

We headed over to the remains of our fire. It looked piddly by comparison to theirs, but it had been a trial run. We needed to build something that would last us all night. Only there was a slight problem.

There had been a load of firewood piled up against one of the walls that ran around the courtyard. Lots of smaller twigs and branches, and some bigger logs. Obviously the others had used some already. There was still quite a few of the smaller bits of wood, but all the logs had gone. It was pretty obvious where.

"Oh ah, it'll be alright," said Flossie, smiling anxiously. "We can still use these small ones to get a fire going. Be nice and cozy in no time."

True, but for how long? We needed those bigger logs if we wanted to have a fire that lasted more than a couple of hours. I was already annoyed by Grayson's sneakiness, now this fuckwittery — I wasn't having it.

I marched over to Golden Boy, leaving the rest of my party to stand and watch from a distance, of course. Had I stopped to think about what I was doing, I wouldn't have done it. Probably would have had a panic attack just at the idea of confronting them. Fortunately for me, I wasn't thinking at all.

"Hey, why did you take all the larger bits of wood? There's none left now." I sounded whiney and like a little bitch, but there was nothing I could do about it now. I was all in.

"Hey, hey, hey," said the big black dude, putting his hands on his hips and 'inadvertently' flexing the huge muscles in his arms. "Easy, bruv. We just took what we needed. Plenty left over."

"Yeah, thanks for leaving us the twigs. I don't know if you understand how weather works, but it gets colder at night. If you want a fire that lasts, you need those larger logs to form a base. What the fuck is wrong with you?"

My little speech designed to imply he must be stupid did its job. His smile dropped and he ran his tongue over his lips.

"You want to watch your mouth, mate. No need to be uncivil."

When a big guy starts talking about good manners, you know he's lining up a punch aimed at your face. But I was in a strange world, trapped with the Noob Squad, facing imminent death by ogres of one kind or another. I was too pissed off to back down.

"Really? You think taking more than your fair share and leaving others to freeze is civil behaviour? Take what you want and the hell with everyone else, that's your idea of being a decent human being? Your mum would be proud of you, would she?" I threw in the mother thing because all the black guys I've ever known held their mothers in high regard. To a ridiculous degree in some cases. Racist stereotype? Possibly, but when you're up against a guy who can crush your skull with his bare hands, you don't really have time to consider all the politically correct ramifications.

"Guys, come on, calm down." Golden Boy had decided to take charge of the situation. "We only took a little extra because there's more of us."

"There's six of you, and five of us. That's one more

person, out of twenty. Does it look like you took an extra one-twentieth?" I pointed at the bonfire of the vanities raging behind him.

"Okay," said Golden Boy, "maybe we overdid it, but we didn't mean any harm. We aren't trying to deprive you guys. You're all welcome to come over here and share the fire with us. How about it?"

He looked past me at the rest of my group over by our area. His smile was big and magnanimous and it made me want to puke. I could sense the others walking over towards us. I'd look pretty silly if they all agreed to share the fire and only I held out. A compromise would probably be the best thing. If you think that's what I went with, you obviously don't know me at all.

"How about it? How about fuck you? You did a shitty thing and now you've been called on it, instead of giving back what you stole, you're trying to wheedle out a way so you keep what you took."

"Jesus," said the black guy, sounding like he was right on the edge. "We invited you to join us, what more do you want?"

"Yeah, an invitation to join a bunch of thieving arseholes. No thanks." The others were now standing behind me. I was just waiting for one of them to suggest we agree to share, so I could tell them they could go fuck themselves too. But they didn't say anything. Whether because they were backing me up or just too nervous to speak, it's hard to say.

"You know," said the black guy, "I've had just about enough of you." He moved his hand along his waist.

I noticed their weapons for the first time. The black guy had an axe. Only a small one, a hatchet I guess, but it looked like it could do some serious damage. Golden Boy had a sword. Yes, a real sword. I don't think he got it from the handouts earlier, so he must have found it or bought it.

"Easy, Dag," said Golden Boy. "No need for that."

"Come on, Tin, he's asking for it."

"Dag and Tin?" said Maurice. "What are you two supposed to be, Teletubbies?"

crickets

I started sniggering. I couldn't help it. Not at Maurice's terrible attempt at a cutting slam, but at the way it totally killed the conversation. Everyone just stared at him.

I patted him on the shoulder. "Nice try, man."

He shook his head, looking more upset about the premature death of his stand-up comedy career than the life-threatening beating we were on the verge of receiving.

"Tough crowd," he muttered under his breath.

Maurice's intervention did have one good side-effect. It lifted the red mist and made me realise you don't beat arseholes by acting like one.

"Look," I said, "once we get out of this place, you can do what you want. Kill us all in a fair fight if you want. You with your swords and axes, us with our sticks and stones. I'm sure the girls will all be very impressed."

The three girls in their party, including Jenny, had been watching silently. I decided to include them because a guy will act differently when he's in front of girls. He wants them to believe he's cool and brave and whatever other bullshit he thinks will get him laid.

"But while we're in here," I continued, "it would be nice if you let us do what we want instead of stealing our options. We want to build our own fire, our own way. Do you think you could stop cockblocking us?"

"Fine," said Golden Boy, whose name was Tin (short for Justin?). "Help yourself." He stepped aside.

The heat from the fire made your face melt if you looked at it too long. The flames crackled and popped, and the centre glowed crimson like a warning light. Getting the burning logs out of that seemed like a fool's errand. The job I was born for.

I raised my stick, letting them see its barbed end for a moment (I enjoyed seeing their eyes widen as they realised I wasn't quite so defenseless as they'd thought) before smacking it into the fire. I felt the nails dig into wood and pulled.

A large log, bathed in flames, came skidding out. At the same time, the rest of the fire collapsed. Logs rolled out, the roasting pig fell, burning twigs went flying. Everyone jumped back, squealing and swearing as they tried to avoid getting hit by red-hot embers.

I ignored the protests and hooked out some more logs.

"For fuck's sake! Look what you've done, bruv." Dag sounded extremely hacked off. "It's ruined!"

The pig was lying in the dirt, a couple of burning branches on top searing the flesh.

"What? He told me to help myself. If you want to blame someone—" I pointed at Tin "—blame him for being a cocky wanker. Anyway, the pig looks fine. Just think of it as barbecue."

I kicked the log nearest me so it rolled over to our area. The others followed my lead and kicked and poked the still-burning wood away from the murderous looks aimed our way.

17. Then There Were Three

Getting a fire going was pretty easy since the logs were already smouldering nicely. We piled them together, added a few smaller bits of wood, and hey presto.

We focused on getting the rabbit cleaned and organising a way to cook it. I could feel eyes on us, but made sure not to respond. There was no doubt in my mind that the issue was not over yet. At some point we would be made to pay for my outburst, but for the time being I intended to eat dinner and plan for tomorrow.

It's worth mentioning that while out little dispute was ongoing, the Cool Kids totally ignored us. I don't mean they watched quietly, I mean I don't think they even noticed. Whatever they were talking about must have been far more important and interesting than what us plebs got up to.

Cooking the rabbit was kind of tricky without utensils. Although we'd probably find out later that Captain Grayson had a drawer full of spoons, forks, pots and pans. I emptied my stew into one of the other dishes and placed my dish on top of the fire. Thanks to Flossie's knife, cutting up the rabbit wasn't too hard. I placed the chunks on the dish like it was a hot plate and let them sizzle away.

My spike with the handle worked well as a tool to take bits of rabbit off the hot plate, but you had to be quick.

We impaled the main body onto Maurice's metal rod and balanced it (rather precariously) on posts hammered into the ground. Turning it so the flames cooked it evenly took some doing, and it fell into the fire a couple of times. But it tasted quite good, if a little plain.

Together with the stew, we had quite a filling meal. It

also helped that Dudley came up with the idea of whittling some of the firewood into crude spoons using Flossie's knife. We sat around the fire stuffing our faces.

Darkness crept up on us, revealing a stunning sky of stars. Was it different to our own sky? I have no idea. I didn't recognise any constellations, but then I probably wouldn't back home either. In London, where I lived, the city lights made it hard to see the night sky properly. Plus it was London, so heavy rain clouds were the norm. I did think maybe there'd be two or three moons up there, but there weren't any.

We lay on our blankets, staring up at the glittering sky, which definitely seemed to be stuffed to overfilling with pinpoints of light.

The other groups settled down for the night, and one thing became apparent. There were only three groups now. The four girls hadn't returned, and it didn't look like they were coming back.

My first thought was that they were dead. They met some monster, or some unsavory people, and were killed. I didn't know if that's what happened to them, and it might be a bit presumptuous to assume they couldn't take care of themselves just because they were girls, but if any group had failed to come back, I would think the same thing.

On the other hand, maybe they ran into a band of handsome knights and got invited back to their castle for tea and crumpets. Even the most strident feminazi might find that a hard offer to turn down.

Whatever their fate, we didn't talk about it, even though I'm sure everyone noticed.

One by one the others drifted off to sleep. It had been a long day — hard to believe it was still only our first — but I lay there with my eyes wide open. Partly because I worried about a sneak attack when we were all asleep, but mainly because I felt too anxious to rest.

I've never been able to fall asleep in a car or a train or even on a plane when they turn off all the cabin lights and give you a pillow and blanket. The idea of the vehicle crashing, no matter how unlikely it might seem, always keeps me up. I felt like that as I lay by a dying fire in a strange world. The crash could come at any moment.

I got up to add some more fuel to the fire and chanced a look over at Golden Boy's group. Or should I say Tin's group. They had managed to rebuild their fire, and while it wasn't as big as before, it was still bigger than ours. They were all huddled together, boys and girls leaning against each other under blankets. All except for one. Jenny sat a little apart, arms around her knees.

I looked away, but that image of her stayed with me. It would be the last I'd see of her for a long time.

18. Good Hunting

I must have dropped off at some point. When I woke up, the others were pottering around the fire. It was early, cold and bright. Our group was the only one in the courtyard.

"Where'd the rest of them go?" I asked, worried we had missed another memo.

"No idea," said Maurice. "They were already gone when I woke up."

At least it meant we wouldn't have to deal with any awkwardness. We got our stuff together, did our business in the bathroom — which, as expected, was a hole in the ground — and set off for the hunting grounds.

We were much more confident in what we had to do, and more relaxed about it. Even Dudley joined in the conversations about who would bag the most rabbits, although he still had a habit of looking straight up when he spoke.

We seemed to reach our destination a lot quicker this time, but I think familiarity with our surroundings just made it feel like that. The rabbits were waiting for us and as unimpressed with our deadly intentions as they were the day before. And with good reason.

Our aiming still left a lot to be desired, but there was some improvement. We would hit the target more often, but they weren't kills. Even though the stones flew out at considerable speed, a headshot was the only way to really kill them. Otherwise they limped off. You might think injured bunnies might be easier to catch, but you'd be wrong.

We came up with a plan to all target the same rabbit. The idea was, if we got a couple of hits in that might be enough to slow it down enough to close in for the kill with my club. It didn't quite work out that way, but the club did turn out to be the key.

Instead of going after them, we decided to bring them to us. I stood in one spot while the others herded the rabbits towards me. As they scampered past me, I lashed my club through the crowd like a wild golf swing. I couldn't miss. And my club held onto what it hit, even if it didn't kill. A quick stab with my spike-handle and it was goodnight and sweet dreams.

This also gave Maurice a new idea, one to rival his bicycle enterprise.

"All this open space," he said, looking around us. "It's like a fairway, isn't it? You could build a pretty good golf course here."

That's right, he wanted to introduce golf to this world. Teaching them the most boring game ever invented could be seen as a form of revenge for what this world had put us through, but other than that I didn't really see the point.

"You think people around here have a lot of free leisure time? 'I'll milk the cows later, love. Just off to the club for a quick back nine'?"

"It is the game of kings," said Dudley. I waited for him to continue, but that was it. Back to sky-staring.

We got three more rabbits in quick succession before they got wise to us and ran off in different directions, making sure to avoid me. But then we switched who had the club and they fell for it again.

We stopped around lunch time and built a fire from scratch. Took a while, but we did it. We also skinned the rabbits. Which was not fun.

You expect these things to be hard at first, but the reality was more brutal than any expectation. We struggled to get their fur off in one piece and gutting them was also not a good time. But we did it and had rabbit kebabs for lunch (quite a late lunch by the time we finished).

The other rabbits watched impassively, not at all perturbed by their brethren roasting over an open fire.

By the time we decided to head back we had ten rabbits, all skinned and one eaten.

We went to the tanner and handed over the skins. He bought eight of them, which was generous. Two had been ripped to shreds but another three were also far from perfect. We got our hands on money for the first time.

Eight chobs. They were small black discs. Very light and smooth. They had no markings on them and almost felt like plastic. Maybe enamel.

We also visited the butcher and tried to sell him some of our rabbits. He was a chubby man with a sweaty face. He looked at our offerings, shook his head and shooed us off. I had no idea what the issue with rabbit meat was, but clearly it wasn't a popular part of the local diet.

As we were wondering what to do with all the rabbit meat, I caught the eye of a guy running one of the food stalls — the one selling grilled meat. He surreptitiously waved me over and then opened a cabinet under his cart. He didn't say anything, just nodded his head to indicate we stick the rabbits in there.

He gave us five chobs for eight rabbits (we kept one for ourselves). I have no idea if that was a fair price, but I was glad to get rid of them.

We went shopping, but thirteen chobs didn't buy much. We got two sacks which would help carry stuff around. A needle and thread, which I insisted would come in useful, although I hadn't decided how. And some salt. There was only so much bland food I could take.

We returned to the shed and found we had the courtyard to ourselves. We built a fire, being sure to leave enough for the others, but we needn't have worried. The other two groups didn't return that night.

19. Let's Get Salty

Salt. Holy shit. For one chob, we'd got a small bag of salt that would last us weeks. One pinch was enough to season a plate of food. You can keep your crack cocaine and your black tar heroin. That night's rabbit stew blew our minds.

After we ate, it became clear the other groups had moved on. Levelled up. Cleared the final boss. Found a way to Stage 2. Who knows? They were gone, and we were still here.

We threw some extra logs on the fire just for the hell of it and considered our next move.

"From tomorrow," I said, "we're really going to have to start grinding those rabbits."

"Ugh!" said Flossie. "Why?"

"No," I said. "What I mean is, we have to kill a lot more and as quickly as possible. It's going to be a grind, like how a boring job is a grind, but it's the best way for us to make money without too many risks. Once we can afford better equipment, we can think about hunting more rewarding beasts."

They all nodded knowingly. Two days in and they were all veterans. Sadly, rabbits were not going to prepare us for the things waiting out there. Apparently, that was my job.

"We're definitely getting better, but we're still too slow and too hesitant. We need to be merciless with those rabbits, and with anything else we might run into. So far we've been lucky. We haven't encountered any monsters, but that can change any minute. We need to be prepared."

Nods all round again. I guess it was better than them arguing with me about the rights of monsters to live a peaceful life, eating who they please.

"We're still weak and our gear is... unreliable. Getting good with weapons doesn't happen overnight. It takes months, years even. What we need is better teamwork. The way we got all those rabbits in the end wasn't with our super ninja skills, it was teamwork, right?"

The nods were more enthusiastic. They were onboard with my message of mutual cooperation and positivity. You're probably thinking, how wonderful. Finally they're coming together. With the power of friendship these guys have a chance of making it. But then, sometimes what you think is happening, isn't what's actually happening.

"We have to trust each other. Rely on each other. We can't get depressed and all self-doubty because we're afraid others might not like us. There are no others here. It's just us, and none of us is perfect. Far from it. Which is why I think we should all just admit our fears, our weaknesses. If everybody already knows what you're worried they might find out, what have you got to lose? Nothing, right?"

They looked less sure with their nods this time. Their heads bobbed ambiguously, like maybe they were agreeing, maybe they got caught by a breeze.

"I'll start. I tend to push people away. You might have noticed. I like to reject them before they reject me, because that's what usually happens, and it doesn't feel good. So I do it first and I'm much happier that way. Or at least less unhappy. Of course, if someone really wants to be friends with me, they'll resist when I push them away. No one ever has. So that's me."

I looked expectantly at them, letting my gaze pass from one to the next. Nothing. No one spoke or looked like they were going to. I kept going.

"Even you lot, I fully expect you to eventually to go off on your own once you feel a bit more confident. Which is fine, I'll just go back to being on my own. I'm used to it."

Still nothing. I wondered how far I'd have to go to get these guys to open up.

Then Claire said, "I have a boyfriend back home." Everyone stared at her, but she was focused on the fire. "He's not very nice to me. In fact, he's a bastard. Tells me I'm ugly, that no one else would have me, makes fun of me in front of his friends." Her voice started to break up a little. "Sometimes I get upset with him, scream at him, tell him to fuck off. But I always take him back."

"Why?" I asked her.

She looked at me across the fire. "Because he's right. And I'd rather be with someone than no one."

Nobody said anything for a while.

I scratched my chin, the stubble reminding me I hadn't shaved, or brushed my teeth or combed my hair in an age. "Claire, I don't know what will happen to us, but I think I can guarantee that none of us will abandon you because of the way you look." There were murmurs of agreement from around the fire. "Your personality, maybe, but not your loo—"

I ducked as a stick came hurtling at me.

"Fuck you," said Claire, but there was laughter in her voice.

"Oh, ah, erm," began Flossie. "People think of me as happy because ahm always smiling and that. But the truth is, people get me to do things for them, and never do anything for me in return." She laughed. "It's kind of depressing really. Even my own family. I guess I'm a bit of a doormat." She laughed again. It was a hollow, joyless laugh. "The nicer I am, the more I do for them, the worse it gets." She smiled a sad-eyed smile. "I don't know what else I can do to make them like me."

Claire put her arm around her and whispered something in Flossie's ear, which brought a slightly more genuine smile to her lips. I turned to Dudley. He immediately looked up at the sky. I was about to move on when he spoke.

"I've always been something of a disappointment to my parents. They sent me to the finest schools, bought me everything I could possibly want or need. And yet, I've never been able to live up to their expectations. I just don't have it in me. I try, I really do, but my mind wanders, I lose track and before I know it, I've failed again. I hope I don't let you down too."

Word of encouragement flew around the fire.

"I'm black," said Maurice. As revelations go, this one didn't come as a big shocker. "But I don't like hip-hop and I consider R&B music to be the work of paedophiles."

Flossie raised her hand. Nobody had mentioned a Q and A segment, but Maurice gave her a nod.

"Ah like R. Kelly," she said. "He's good."

"There's no point," said Maurice. "You're too old for him."

"What about the 'Remix of Ignition'?" said Claire. "I like that tune."

Flossie agreed.

"Hot and fresh out the kitchen," threw in Dudley in his incredibly plummy voice.

Maurice looked over at me, somewhat baffled. I shrugged.

"My point," continued Maurice, "is that other black people have never accepted me. They think I'm trying to be something I'm not. Whereas actually they're the ones trying to force me to pretend. And of course, white people aren't keen to have someone on their turf either, so I'm something of an outsider. I mean, my parents have tried to reach out to me, but they don't know how to relate to me. Last Christmas my mother got me..." He started to choke up. "She got me a Maroon 5 CD." Pain flashed behind his eyes. "She meant well. She meant well."

"What kind of music do you like?" I asked him, genuinely curious.

"Oh, Rage Against The Machine, Nine Inch Nails, any quality rock really."

What the fuck?

"Maurice, before you got transported here, when you were back on Earth, what year was it?"

He pushed his glasses back up his face. "2016. Why?"

"Nothing. Just surprised you listen to those bands."

"Timeless music is timeless," he said.

Each to his own, I guess. In any case, I had a better idea of who I was dealing with now. Of course, what I said about myself was utter horseshit. I didn't reject people because I thought they'd reject me. I could care less. Oh, you're thinking, poor guy's in denial. Can't admit the truth. Maybe, but if I am in denial, then I have no idea I'm kidding myself (that's why it's called *denial*) so either way, it isn't something I waste time getting worked up about. The only reason I'd said it was to get the ball rolling. Now I knew their insecurities and weaknesses, it would be much easier to manipulate and control them.

Not that I intended to use the knowledge in a malicious way, but if I didn't get them into some kind of decent fighting force, we'd all be dead by the weekend, assuming the concept of weekends existed here. And if it didn't, I'm sure Maurice would attempt to invent it.

20. Equipment Upgrade

As the others sat around the fire, smiling at each other, talking freely, you could see the bonds forming between them. Loyalty, concern, affection. All beautiful symbols of friendship, and all next to useless.

You might think a party who are willing to die for each other would provide a powerful advantage in a fight. But the aim isn't to die, it's to stay alive.

What I needed from them was obedience, focus and an unwavering desire to win. Fat chance of getting those qualities out of this lot.

"Get all our equipment out, I'll be back in a minute." If it sounds like I was talking down to them, acting like I was in charge, that's not how it was. They did as I asked not because I was the leader, but because they had started to trust me. They hadn't just bonded with each other, they had bonded with me as well. We were in this together. Or at least that's how they saw it.

I saw it in more practical terms. I had to tell them what to do because otherwise they might start thinking for themselves, and then we'd really be in trouble. I know that probably sounds quite arrogant. With me at the helm, we'd be winners in no time! Stage cleared. Flawless victory. No, I didn't think that. Our survival chance weren't good no matter who gave the orders. I was just the lesser of five evils.

Plus, the truth was I feared the future. The other groups had found a way to progress and we were way behind. Not that turning on my companions would benefit our cause, but I was edgy as fuck and snapping at people was my coping mechanism. Not a good mechanism, just the only one I had.

I went into the shed where Grayson was sitting at the desk, writing in a ledger of some kind. He used a stick of what looked like charcoal to write with. I couldn't make head or tail of what he was writing, it was in the strange script that looked like squiggles.

He looked up questioningly.

"Is it alright if I take some of this stuff?" I pointed at the box with the last of the clothes in it.

He nodded. "Tomorrow will be the last day here for us. And for you. We'll be shutting everything up and going back to the city. You'll be on your own."

I had forgotten we'd only been promised three days of care. Or, I hadn't forgotten, but I had put it out of my mind. Now it was front and centre, and I only felt worse.

"Do you come here every four years?" I asked him.

"Not me. At least I hope not. Some other poor bastard who's fallen out of favour with the powers that be."

So this was considered a shit detail, assigned to whoever had pissed his superiors off the most. Grayson did look the type.

"Who is it you work for, exactly?"

"The National Alliance." He pointed at the map on the wall. "You remember the four cities I mentioned before? They're each responsible for their own province, but for larger matters there's a council, the National Alliance, which has representatives from each city. I act under their purview."

There were probably many more questions I could have asked about this world, how it was run, who was in charge... but Grayson did not give off a chatty vibe. I felt like I was being a huge imposition just breathing the same air as him.

"By the way, do you know what happened to the other groups?"

Grayson gave a noncommittal shrug. It could have

meant he didn't know, or that he wasn't going to tell me. Or possibly that his shoulders ached and he wanted to go to bed. It was evening, and the soldiers tended to disappear once it got dark. I had no idea where to. There was a lot I didn't know.

My gaze wandered over to the curtain I had only recently become aware of. I'd have liked to had a look in the alcove behind, see what other hidden treasures might be back there, but I doubted Grayson would allow it. He was already back to his writing as though I wasn't even there.

I grabbed everything from the clothes box and returned to the courtyard. The others had spread our gear out in front of the fire. A paltry collection.

I handed a woollen tank top, too small for even the girls, to Dudley. "Can you pick that apart? We can use the wool as thread for the needle." We did have some thread, but I already had plans for it. Plus it wouldn't be good for heavy duty stuff, which the wool might. Maybe.

"Can someone thread this needle?" I held up the sewing kit we had bought earlier. Claire took it from me. "By the way, can either of you sew?"

Both girls gave me that look modern girls like to throw around when you say something that could be perceived as sexist. The one that says, "What do I look like? Your mother?" Which is hugely unreasonable. since my mother is also a modern girl and totally useless when it comes to household stuff.

"I'm just asking, a simple yes or no would do."

Claire shook her head but Flossie said, "Little bit."

"Okay, great." I handed the rest of the clothes to Maurice. "Can you cut these into strips? We can sew them to the sacks to make them easier to carry. The rest we can wrap around some sticks to make torches. We'll probably need light in a dark place at some point."

I went over to the woodpile and selected a few suitable sticks for the torches, and also retrieved the collection of junk I'd got from the smithy that I'd stashed there. I didn't think they would get stolen, I hid them so no one would mistake them for trash and throw them away. Now that we had needle and thread, I could attempt making a sap by sewing the bits of metal inside a piece of leather.

If this were a movie, we'd be putting all this stuff together in a montage with cool music over it. The heroes prepare for action. In real life it probably looked more like we were sorting out the recycling for the bin men.

21. Shrek 2

I had a plan. Wait until it gets late and Grayson and his boys go off to wherever they went to at night, then ransack the shed for every secret hidden behind the curtain and in the desk drawers. Excellent plan, I think we can all agree.

Unfortunately, the moment I put my head down to give my eyes a rest, I was out like a light. Whether my body was getting used to being in this place or I was just knackered, the next thing I knew, it was morning.

We were woken by Grayson banging a spoon on a dish (I knew the bastard had spoons hidden somewhere!).

"Good morning," he boomed cheerfully. "Looks like it's going to be another beautiful day. Sunshine and fresh air aplenty."

We groggily got up, faces squishy and eyes glued shut. The fire was dead, and it looked like the last two days of constant fear and anxiety had wiped us all out.

"Now, I do want to remind those of you left, I and my men will be leaving today. You'll need somewhere else to sleep, and you'll have to take care of your other needs yourself from now on. However, we won't set off until after dark, so if you do have anything you need to ask, you've got until then."

I got the impression he would have liked to have left earlier, but he was delaying the departure to give us every opportunity to do... something. Ask a question, hand in a token, claim a prize — I didn't know what it was we were supposed to do, I just knew we were supposed to do something, which most likely the other groups had already done.

"Do you have anything you want to ask me now?" He

looked at each of us in turn.

Nobody said anything. We were all still half asleep, but I'm not sure that was the problem. I could sense this was more or less our last chance, but my brain refused to offer up any ideas.

"Okay then. Good luck." The way he said it made it sound like he knew we'd be needing it. He turned around and went back inside.

I felt pretty scuzzy. I hadn't had a proper wash in days, and my clothes needed cleaning. There was a hand pump in the corner of the courtyard that provided our water, but we didn't have soap or towels, plus we were too shy to undress in front of each other. You also needed someone to work the pump for you so you could use both hands.

All stuff we should be able to work out between us, but hadn't.

Not knowing when we'd be able to find a decent water supply again, I stripped down to my rank-smelling boxers and asked Maurice to pump the water for me. He agreed, of course, making it seem completely stupid I hadn't just asked on day one.

The water was freezing cold. I got down on all fours and stuck my head under the spigot to wash my hair and as much of my body as I could. I wasn't about to stick my hand down my shorts and give things a good scrub with all the people around (although God knows I needed to), but getting everything wet helped with the smell at least.

I operated the pump for Maurice, although he didn't have anything on under his onesie, so he had to go nude. The girls had tactfully disappeared into the shed, making it less embarrassing, but we still took great care not to make eye contact or any other kind of contact.

Yes, we were those guys. The ones who can't handle communal showers and can't piss at a urinal if someone's standing next to us. I realise it's retarded, but we'd each had a couple of decades of feeling shit about ourselves, we weren't going to undo all of it overnight.

Dudley was the tallest and had the most difficulty getting low enough to wash properly, but he did the best he could by splashing water over himself. We used the blankets as makeshift towels and patted ourselves dry.

Once dressed, and only slightly damp, we went into the shed where the girls were eating the fruit provided us for breakfast. While we ate, the girls went off to wash themselves, a tacit understanding between us that we wouldn't enter the courtyard until they were done.

Grayson was at his desk doing more paperwork, so I couldn't have a look behind the curtain unless I rushed past him and yanked it open. Which I totally could have done — it wasn't like he'd kill me for it — but I couldn't make myself do it. I stood there, sweaty with indecision.

After we'd washed and eaten, we put all our gear in the sacks which now had straps on them so you could carry them like backpacks. One had the blankets in it, the other had metal dishes and the homemade torches. It had taken us ages to get everything ready, the sewing being particularly difficult and painful. Flossie had done most of it, but I had stitched together a very poorly constructed sap, and my fingers still stung from the effort. You really had to force the needle through the leather.

I wasn't too impressed with the results, the YouTube video I had seen made the simple weapon seem much more impressive. But then, all I'd done was stuff various bits of metal into a triangle of leather, sewn around the edges and sewn on a thin piece of leather as a strap. By looping the strap over your wrist and holding one end of the triangle, you could strike someone quite sharply while giving the impression you were just slapping them, which might work well as a surprise attack. But the metal needed to be heavier to have any real effect. Still, it would be more effective than a punch and less likely to break my knuckles.

All geared up and ready to face the day, we set off for our regular hunting ground. I couldn't shake the feeling I was missing something and that Grayson was giving us one last chance to figure it out. We had the rest of the day to think about it, but after that he'd be gone for good and we'd be on our own.

We headed for the wheatfields, practicing with our slings and talking about rabbit hunting strategies. No matter how uncertain I felt on the inside, I couldn't show it. If the others lost confidence, in themselves or me, we wouldn't stand a chance. So far things had gone alright, but it would only take one bad experience to wreck us.

I mentioned my thoughts on Grayson waiting for us to ask him something, and the others agreed it seemed like that. But when I asked them if they could think of any questions, there was the usual deafening silence.

"We've got the rest of the day to come up with something," I said. "Try to think about it. We should try to get as much info out of him as we can before he leaves."

They all nodded and made thoughtful faces, but I didn't hold out much hope. If I was going to figure out what Grayson wanted from us, I was probably going to have to do it alone.

"Also, I've been thinking, we need to make plans for particular eventualities." They looked at me like I was talking a foreign language. Apart from Dudley, who looked straight up as usual. "For example, if we run into trouble that we can't handle and you hear someone shout 'Run!', then we need to have sorted out where we run to, beforehand."

Plenty of nods, no comments.

"If something happens today—" nervous looks zigzagged around me "—I'm not saying it will, just if, then our meeting point will be back in town. But only shout it if you mean it. No joking around with this sort of thing. You hear 'Run!' and you peg it. Don't wait to find out what's going on. No questions. Grab what you can and start running."

"Shouldn't we leave everything?" asked Claire. "If it's dangerous, it'll only slow us down."

"No. We have fuck all as it is, we can't afford to lose any of it. I mean, don't stop to pack things up and put them away. But if it's within reach, take it. And generally keep things within reach and assume you may have to run at any moment."

It's probably great when a team's been together awhile, with their own shorthand way of communicating and an innate understanding of their roles in any given scenario. But when you've known each other for three days, you have to have conversations where you state the blindingly obvious.

"And when you run, really run. Don't stop. Don't go back. If someone's in trouble, getting yourself in trouble too won't help."

There was some grumbling at that.

"Look, if you want to go back and help someone who's fallen and can't get up, that's your choice. I can't stop you. What I'm saying, though, is if you're the person who's fallen, don't automatically assume we're coming back for you. You need to save yourself. That's the mindset you need. Fireman Sam will not be coming to the rescue, and the rest of us may have our own problems to contend with."

They seemed to see the value of what I was saying, although how much they'd remember when the shit hit the fan, I had no way of knowing.

We made it to the other side of the wheatfield and

headed up the slope. With no shade, the sun bore down on us as we climbed to the top. Already out of breath, we were met by a gentle breeze and the sight of an ogre.

It was sitting in the middle of our meadow, crouched down on its haunches. It was about the same size as the one in the woods we'd encountered on our first day, but it had lighter coloured hair. It also gave off a completely different vibe just sitting there. It was still terrifying, but without the roaring and thrashing about, it didn't make you want to scream yourself hoarse. It made you want to keep very quiet and hope it didn't notice you.

What was really strange, though, was how the rabbits were reacting. They had gathered around the ogre in a circle, pushing each other out of the way to get closer.

The ogre reached down and placed the back of its hand on the grass. The rabbits immediately swarmed onto its palm. The ogre lifted the mass of squirming fur to its mouth and shovelled them in like popcorn. You'd think this might upset a few of the rabbits below. They couldn't have not noticed. But they actually tried even harder to get closer. "Me next!" they seemed to be saying. The ogre obliged.

We all watched, transfixed, as more rabbits eagerly jumped onto the proffered hand and disappeared down its gullet. We were far enough away that we weren't in immediate danger, but if it saw us and decided to attack, were we really ready to deal with it?

No. Not even close.

"Hey," I whispered to get the others' attention. "Run." I turned and ran, not waiting to see if my earlier comments had sunk in.

22. Choose Your Own Adventure

Running away felt good. Partly because the distance between me and the monster was getting bigger, and partly because it always feels good running downhill.

You might think it was a missed opportunity. The ogre had no idea we were there, the ideal chance for a sneak attack. What a prize we might have claimed! Yeah, well, death ain't much of a prize. The problem is, you can't understand what it's like to see an actual monster.

Imagine if you walked into your living room and a gorilla was sitting in your favourite chair. You'd shit yourself, right? Now imagine the gorilla ten times bigger, with the face of the uncle who molested you when you were a kid, and you're in the ballpark. Oh, you didn't have an uncle like that? Sure, and you think I'm the one in denial.

I didn't stop till I was back in town. I zoomed around the wheatfield and didn't slow down as I approached the buildings. Not once did I look back to see if the others were following. If they couldn't understand basic instructions, what hope was there for them?

Gasping for breath, I finally came to a stop outside the shed, where one of the soldiers stood by the door doing nothing in particular. He watched me come racing up with a quizzical look on his face. I didn't know his name and had never spoken to him, but I felt the urge to explain myself for some reason.

"Training session," I said, panting for air. "Keeping fit."

He nodded, turned and went inside. I don't know why I even bother.

Claire and Maurice came jogging round the corner next, followed by Flossie and Dudley. We'd decided to take turns carrying the sacks, and the girls had them on when we reached the meadow. The boys had them on now. They must have stopped to switch. Perfect gentlemanly behaviour, the kind that could get you killed. Well, at least they made it back.

"Good," I said. "You all remembered the plan."

Red-faced and out of breath, Claire put her hands on her hips. "He didn't see us. We didn't have to run all the way."

"Yes we did," I said. "When we make a plan, we need to stick to it. Today turned out okay, but next time might not go so smoothly. That's why always doing exactly what we decide is vital."

Was this true? No. Changing plans on the fly as circumstances dictate is the wise move. If you have the sense to adapt appropriately, that is. If you don't have the sense, or any sense, then under no circumstances should you think for yourself. You will get yourself killed, or worse, you will get me killed.

"What now?" asked Maurice, doubled over and breathing hard.

Our plan to farm the shit out of the rabbit population had gone up in smoke. No way could we risk going back to the meadow, and even if we did, there probably wouldn't be any rabbits left. Other options included hunting pigs or dogs, but we didn't even know where to start looking for them, never mind coming up with a strategy how to hunt them.

"Ah, you're back," said Grayson as he emerged from the shed. "One of my men mentioned you were out here."

The guy I spoke to obviously thought I'd run back to ask Grayson important things about how to be a first class adventurer. Awkward.

"Ah, yes," I said, trying to stall. "We were wondering about... magic. Are there any spells you can teach us?"

Grayson shook his head. "I'm afraid not."

"Do you have books that we can learn skills from?" More head shaking. "What about weapons? Are there some secrets to fighting you can share? Is there some place we should visit? Someone we need to talk to?"

Every question got the same response. I looked to the others to help me out.

"Er…" began Maurice. "Has anyone invented the bicycle yet?"

"I… don't… think so." Grayson clearly had no idea what Maurice was talking about.

"If there's something we need to know, can't you just tell us?" I was quite exasperated by this point and ready to admit defeat.

"I'm afraid it doesn't work like that. If I help you now, you'll just fall at the next hurdle. It does you no good in the long run."

"Fine," I snapped at him. "Can you at least tell us where to find pigs?"

He seemed a bit surprised at my sudden change of tone, but I'd had enough of his well-meaning but useless bullshit. If we were going to be forced to do everything for ourselves, there was no point in being nice to him.

"You can find wild boar in the forest, back where we found you. Be careful though, they're unfriendly bastards."

"Isn't everyone?" I didn't wait for a reply and walked away.

The others followed. I didn't bother discussing where we were going. If they didn't agree, they could stop following me. It took them until we were approaching the trees before someone spoke. That's a full hour of walking, around the wheatfield in the other direction and over a small stream I had no recollection of crossing when we first travelled to town, although we must have.

"Are we going to hunt pigs in there?" asked Maurice. "Because I'm not sure the best way to do that. Will our slings even work?"

"We aren't going to hunt pigs," I said. "I want to go back to the clearing where we first arrived. I want to see if there's anything we missed. Be silly if we spent all this time struggling to get from one day to the next, and the whole time there's a way home just through here." I pointed into the dark, foreboding interior of the forest. "You don't have to come if you don't want to."

They started discussing what to do. I left them to it and walked into the woods not giving a damn. Yes, danger lurked in every shadow, but so what? Danger lurked in every sunlit meadow, too.

Five steps in, and my attitude started to change.

Unlike the last time I was here, this time I was much more aware of the surroundings. Without the disorienting confusion of finding myself in a strange world and the shock of seeing a real live ogre, I was able to appreciate the full dank grandeur of the forest. The scuffling going on behind shrubs, the scuttling around my feet, the dark shapes disappearing up tree trunks — it was all creepy as fuck.

"Hey, wait up!" called Maurice from behind me.

I turned and realised it would be easy to get lost in this place. If Maurice hadn't been heading towards me, I wouldn't have known which direction I had come from. I took out my spike and gouged a mark in the nearest tree trunk. We would have to leave some kind of trail to follow back.

The others congregated around my location and watched me carve an arrow into bark.

"Do you really think it's a good idea to be in here?" asked Maurice, clearly implying it wasn't.

"Probably not," I answered. "What other option do we

have? If we carry on as we are, we're going to end up stuck in Probet forever. We need to take a chance and hope we get lucky. Or at least that's what I intend to do."

"Okay," said Claire, "but can we not go all the way back to town if we have to run?"

"Sure. If someone says 'Run', then we go to the little stream we passed on the way up. If they yell, 'Ruuuuuuuuuuun', that means big trouble, we go all the way back."

They nodded their agreement.

"Okay, now the next thing, does anyone remember which way the clearing is?"

Nobody had a clue, so I turned to face the dark interior of the forest and set off. One direction seemed as good as any other.

We all chipped off bits of bark as we walked. Not that I thought it would make much difference if we got attacked. Once we were deep inside Mirkwood, any monster we encountered pretty much had dinner sorted. No matter how many marks we left, finding them as we ran in panic would be near impossible. It would only make it more likely for us to lose our footing or plough head first into a tree.

The sounds around us seemed to get louder, although I was probably just becoming more aware of them. Chittering from the branches above. Hissing from the undergrowth. The occasional hoot or caw. A struggle somewhere to the left, a branch breaking somewhere to the right.

I had my club and spike ready. Dudley and Maurice carried the sacks. They had taken permanent ownership of rather than have the girls carry them, which was fine by me. Maurice had his metal rod which he used to beat the bark off trees. Dudley had Flossie's knife. I don't know when that arrangement was made, but it was a damn sight easier to carve arrows on tree trunks with that than his assigned weapon, the bola.

Flossie carried her sling, but I doubted she'd be able to swing it without hitting a tree or branch. Claire had her stick. If we did run into a monster, our main form of attack would be to hope it felt pity for us and committed honourable seppuku.

The dim light made it hard to see very far through the trees. Nothing looked familiar or like it had been disturbed recently. You'd think twenty-plus people traipsing through the woods might leave signs of their passing, but apparently we had been born into this world as ninja. Either that or I was taking us in completely the wrong direction.

I don't know how much time had passed — hard to tell with the canopy hiding the sun — but I was just about ready to give up when I stumbled through some low branches into a wide open space.

The sun blinded me for a moment, but once I adjusted to the brightness, I recognised the tall grass and wildflowers as the glade we had started in.

The others stopped beside me, taking in the idyllic scene. Perfect place for a picnic if it wasn't for the smell. The unmistakable odour of shit.

When the ogre had been killed, it emptied its bowels in violent fashion. You don't forget a smell like that, and the air was still heavy with it. The ogre's body had gone. Perhaps it had been eaten by scavengers, or maybe it had risen from the dead and we now faced the possibility of attack from a zombie ogre. A zogre?

We moved around, trying to spot anything unusual, but nothing stood out. Where had we come from? Had we fallen out of the sky? I'm not sure what I hoped to find. A magic wardrobe that led back home would have been nice. Not that I had much to go home to. No loved ones distressed by my sudden disappearance, no luxurious lifestyle to reclaim.

To be honest, the idea of travelling to a strange fantasy world to fight monsters and find treasure would be the kind of thing I would love to do, but not like this. If I had landed with special skills and an OP weapon, cheat mode on, fair enough, I'm down to play. But trying to navigate this place as the lowliest scrub with a stick in one hand and a metal spike in the other was way too hardcore.

"Shit!" cried out Maurice.

"What is it?" I looked around for signs of trouble.

"No, it's shit. Lots of it."

I walked over to him and saw the shit he was talking about. A large area was covered with a light brown crust. It had been a lot darker when it shot out of the ogre's rear end, but being baked by the sun had turned it to the colour of fresh bread. It had also expanded so it was high as my knee. A giant turd muffin.

"Ah," said Flossie, "is it supposed to move like that?" She pointed at the area nearest her, which was trembling. A bubble began to form.

"It's probably the sun warming up the gas inside. We should probably get back," I said. I don't consider myself an expert in these matters, but it seemed a plausible explanation.

We all stepped back as the bubble grew bigger and bigger. It reached beachball proportions and then it popped, and a rabbit jumped out.

It looked like the rabbits we hunted, except for one thing: the long horn growing out of the centre of its head.

"Fooking hell," said Flossie. "It's a bunny unicorn!"

23. Gotta Catch 'Em All

The bunnicorn sat there, twitching slightly. The grass around the pile of shit had wilted and withered, slimy with shit that hadn't dried out. I thought it might feel exposed out in the open with five strangers standing around. But then, the rabbits back in the meadow never gave a damn about us, and, as it turned out, neither did this one.

It shook its head, pawed at the ground and then lowered its head, aiming the horn at me. It charged.

With all the available targets, why it should decide I deserved to have my ankles gored, I don't know. I guess I'm just lucky.

I took a few stumbling steps backwards as it came at me, then turned and ran.

"Hey, do something!" I called out to the others. They decided to offer me the absolute worst form of help: encouragement.

"Run!"

"Dodge left."

"Don't let it touch you, it's covered in shit."

The rabbits back in the meadow had been slow and listless. This thing was hyper. I headed for the taller grass, hoping I might lose it if it couldn't see, but I could hear the bastard's little feet right behind me. I swerved, I double-backed, I tried to lead it towards the others so it might switch targets, but it honed in on me and only me.

Without realising it, I ran into the shitty area where the ground was wet and slippery. My feet went out from under me and I ended up flat on my back. I tilted my head hoping I'd managed to get away, only to see the vicious furball charging right at me. I rolled to the left, coating myself in ogre faeces, and the bunnicorn slid past. Fortunately, it was no better at keeping its footing on the slick surface than me.

I jumped to my feet and ran for the edge of the clearing. For the first time in days I'd had a proper wash, and only a few hours later I was more filthy than any human in history. Typical. I got to the treeline and spun around. The grass shook as the bunnicorn closed in for the kill, and then it emerged at ramming speed, leaping into the air at waist height. There was no doubt, it was aiming for my balls.

I waited for the last possible moment and then dived out of the way. The bunnicorn smacked horn-first into the tree I had been standing in front of, burying the tip deep into the wood. The bunnicorn hung there, levitating three feet off the ground, pawing wildly at the air but unable to get free.

Three quick steps, a wide swing, and I brought my stick across to hit the bunnicorn as hard as I could. It went flying. I'd like to say it went sailing over the horizon, but it bounced off the next tree and dropped into the undergrowth somewhere outside of the clearing. Still out of bounds, so technically: home run!

Its horn was still stuck in the tree, the end of it red and sticky. I yanked it out. It was lighter than I'd expected, and warm to the touch. From my experience of RPGs, a unicorn horn had magical properties and was often a quest item, so there was a good chance this was worth something.

"Hey, guys, look at this."

The others ignored me. They were all facing the other way, unconcerned about my near-brush with castration. I walked over to see what had their attention.

Bubbles were forming all over the dried-out bed of shit. Twinkling in the sunlight and smelling bad enough to curl the hairs in your nostril, the bubbles burst. Out of each one came another bunnicorn.

They landed on the grass with a flump, looked around, saw one of their own kind staring back, and charged. They would get close to stabbing each other in the face, but a flick of the head and the two horns would clash, knocking both jousters aside.

All over the meadow, the bunnicorns were having little duels.

"Why were they inside the shit?" asked Claire.

"Maybe they live in there," said Maurice.

I had my own theory. The sight of those rabbits willingly jumping down that ogre's throat back in the meadow reminded me about something I learned in biology class. Fruit is delicious because the plant wants them to be eaten. Once it passes through an animal's system, the seed gets shat out in its very own package of ready-to-grow fertiliser. The circle of life, brilliant and disgusting.

Perhaps the rabbits were the same. Being eaten and then encased in shit was part of their life cycle. It also seemed to evolve them, like some horrific version of pokemon. Pikadudu turns into Jigglyturd. I could see why the people in Probet had reacted the way they did whenever we asked them about eating the rabbits.

"I think their horns might be worth collecting." I put the horn I was holding in the sack on Dudley's back. "We should hunt them."

"They look a bit dangerous," said Claire.

"Yeah, we have to be careful. But as long as they're distracted by all this fighting amongst themselves, we should be able to pick a few off."

I walked up behind a bunnicorn focused on one of its fellows. As it prepared to charge, I brought my stick down hard, burying a nail into the top of its head, killing it instantly. All the other bunnicorns stopped what they were doing to look at me. It was not a friendly look. They began herding together.

I took a few steps backwards.

The herd charged.

"Stampede!" I turned and ran.

Even though I was the primary target, the others followed me back into the woods. They didn't really have a choice if they didn't want to be trampled to death by little furry feet. It would have probably been a good idea to check which direction I was running in. It quickly became apparent it wasn't the way we came. Not that I had time to worry about little things like that.

We thrashed our way through a large expanse of shrubbery, getting whipped in the face by twigs and branches. We broke through into an area full of very thin trees with even thinner branches covered in bright green leaves. No time to stop and admire the beauty of nature, we had a ton of shit-covered rabbits with horns after us.

I had thought running through the trees would slow them down, but these bunnies did not respect the laws of physics. They leapt over logs and bounced off trees. They came up alongside us, springing through the air like gazelle. We were flanked right and left, a classic pincer movement.

There was light ahead. The trees started to thin out and I saw a lake ahead. I didn't stop, I ran into the water. Of course, there were probably as many nasty things in the water as there were on land — piranha with antlers, knowing my luck — but beggars can't be choosers. I was up to my waist before I turned around to see where the others were. They had followed me into the water and were wading towards me. All along the bank, the bunnicorns were massing, dozens of the fuckers, waving their horns at us like tiny Zulu warriors. Fortunately, they didn't seem keen on getting wet.

I also noted that Dudley and Maurice had taken off their sacks and were carrying them over their heads to keep the contents dry. I felt a slight twinge of guilt. I always treated them like they were clueless, but they'd done the smart thing even with the threat of being impaled from behind. Would I have had the presence of mind to make sure the blankets and torches didn't get soaked? Probably not. So who was I to look down on them?

Feelings of remorse could wait. First we had to get away.

The lake had little islands on it. Some even had trees growing on them. I waded towards one and clambered onto it. There was enough space for all of us, and we could at least get our bearings and sort out what to do next.

The other pulled themselves out of the water and flopped down next to me. We were all out of breath and soaking wet, although at least my little swim managed to get most of the shit off me. When I had got my breath back and sat up, the bunnicorns had gone. I looked around and realised it wasn't really a lake but a large pond. I could see the shore on other side and more trees beyond it. But that's not what caught my attention.

Kneeling by the water, apparently washing some clothes, was a figure about the size of child, a ten-year-old maybe. But not a child. Not even a human. In fact what it most resembled was a large rat. Covered in white fur. With a tail.

I nudged Maurice next to me and pointed. He slowly pushed himself up onto his elbows and looked in the direction I was indicating. His mouth fell open.

"Is that a rat-woman?"

The rat-person did look like a female. Not because she was doing the laundry (I'm not that sexist), not even because she was wearing a long yellow skirt, like a sarong (men wear them, too), but because of the six breasts on her chest.

The others all sat up and gawked. We were far enough away, and the foliage on the island was thick enough that she couldn't see us unless she had a really good look. Still, I think we all felt like it would be best to keep as quiet as possible.

"Actually," said Dudley in hushed tones, "I'd say more likely a mouse-woman."

"How can you tell?" Maurice whispered back.

"Mice have longer snouts, and their ears are bigger in proportion to their head. In addition to which, rats have naked, scaly tails. That one has a hairy tail."

"*This* is your area of expertise?" I asked him.

Dudley shrugged. "One picks these things up."

I returned my focus on the mouse-woman. She picked up a basket and walked away into the trees. I slipped into the water.

"Where are you going?" said Claire.

"That's a fantasy creature I feel I can deal with. Half my size and no weapons growing out of its head. I'm going to follow her."

"What if there are others? With weapons."

"Then I hope they can't swim."

"Actually," said Dudley, "mice are excellent swimmers."

I ignored Dr Moreau and swam to the other side of the pond. After a few seconds I heard the others drop into the water behind me.

I climbed out of the water and listened carefully for signs of life. The sun was high in the sky, and the air was hot and humid. Sounds of wildlife filled the air. Once everyone was out of the water, we headed off in the direction we'd seen the mouse-woman go, weapons at the ready.

We slowly moved through the trees until we came to a clearing. The mouse-woman was hanging up her washing on a line tied between two trees. They were plain squares of cloth, white and brown, maybe sheets, maybe more sarongs. We watched from behind the trees. She finished, picked up the empty basket and pushed aside some bushes to reveal a hidden cave. She disappeared into it, leaving the swishing foliage in her wake.

Was this the entrance to a dungeon? Had the others found it? Were they deep inside, battling their way through various levels and boss monsters? There was only one way to find out.

24. Prepare to Fight

"Shouldn't we all go in together?" asked Claire.

"No," I said. "I'm going to have a quick look just to see what's in there. If it's okay, then I'll come get the rest of you. If it isn't, then I'll be running when I come out. If I'm running, that's your cue to also start running, got it?"

How brave, how selfless. I planned to investigate this dark, forbidding cave alone — had I suddenly found my true hero's heart? No. I just didn't want them stumbling around in there, attracting attention and getting in my way when I tried to get the hell out.

My intention was to literally stick my head in the cave entrance, see what was in there and see if it looked safe to investigate further, and then call the others over. Heroics would be kept to a minimum. And by minimum, I mean exactly zero.

"Remember, if I run out, don't wait to see what's behind me, don't ask questions or make any noise at all — get in the water and head for the island. If they can swim, at least we'll be able to defend ourselves better there than out in the open. Get there as fast as you can and prepare for battle. Okay?"

"What if you don't come back?" asked Claire.

"Then good luck and I wish you all the best."

I crept out from our hiding spot and tried to cross the open area as quickly and quietly as I could. The bushes in front of the cave did a good job of concealing the entrance, so I hoped they also hid my approach from anyone inside. The hole seemed to have been made in a mound of earth not much taller than me. As I stepped past the bushes and through the entrance, I could feel the ground beneath my feet slope downwards. I had to duck a little to enter, and I remained stooped as I walked down into the gloom unable to see much.

Once the tunnel levelled out, a long, straight passageway stretched out ahead of me with pools of light on the floor. There were no sounds, but the faint whiff of something cooking drifted towards me. It smelled like fish.

The ceiling was higher here, and I could stand up straight. I took another few steps forward, my hands touching the walls on either side. They felt smooth but dusty. Then my right hand fell into empty space. I pulled it back and retreated, my heart racing. I waited for a moment, but nothing happened so I reached out to the edge of the wall. There was some kind of opening, but it was too dark to see where it led.

After my eyes adjusted to the near-darkness, I sensed a small room. Nobody appeared to be in there, or at least that was the impression I had. I got on my hands and knees and crawled halfway through the opening, feeling around. There was some grass and straw in a pile (bedding?). Then something sharp pricked me, making my hiss in pain.

I backed out. Whatever was in there, it was dangerous to explore without any light. In the passageway, I examined my hand to find my finger was bleeding. I pulled a piece of glass out of the cut.

A high pitched laugh — a female giggle, it sounded like — came from further down. As I peered into the distance, looking for signs of someone approaching, I could make out an orange glow. I found myself moving towards it.

As I slowly walked towards the glow, I found three more openings, two on my left and one more on my right. They were also dark and seemed empty, but I decided not to investigate. I quickly crossed one of the pools of light. It was from a hole above that revealed the blue sky.

The passageway wasn't that long, maybe fifty feet, and I wanted to see what was at the end. I admit the size of the female mouse had given me confidence in being able to handle myself in a one on one situation. Maybe even overconfidence. She might not be alone. There was a chance I was about to walk into a colony of mice holding their annual get together. And they might be one of those species where the males are a lot bigger than the females.

The sensible thing would be to go get the others, use the torches we'd made so we could see properly and deal with any problems together. I took a few more steps forward.

I could hear voices, squeaky and talking fast.

"That smells delicious, delicious. What a fine cook you've become, my darling."

I heard the giggle again.

"Oh, you. There's no need for flattery, not after what I let you do last night. I can't believe I agreed to such a thing, you old rascal."

"We all need a hobby. Helps pass the time."

"Sometimes I think you're glad the others are gone. Gives you more time to get up to no good." There was a loud sigh. "I do miss them."

"Now, now, don't be sad. Their replacements will be here soon, only a few more days. Then we'll teach those cowardly humans a lesson for taking our boys from us. They will not be forgiven!"

I was close to the end of the tunnel now, my back pressed against the wall. The orange glow was coming from a fire pit, which had a metal pot hanging over it. The female mouse was crouched next to it, stirring the pot. Beside her stood another mouse, but male. He was about the same size as her, maybe a little shorter, but broader. He looked old. He had a white beard and a walking stick he leaned on as he inspected the contents of the pot.

"Back, back," said the female. "It isn't ready yet."

He backed off. "Well, I suppose I'll go get things ready for later. Ha ha, I've thought up a new position for you, I can't wait to try it out." He started to move in my direction. I hurriedly backed off and ducked into one of the openings as he walked past the end of the tunnel to the other side of the room.

I switched sides and pressed my back against the tunnel wall in time to see the male mouse's head peeking out from a trap door in the ground.

"Call me when it's ready, my darling. I'm ravenous — for the food and for you." He said it with a flourish that earned him more giggles and then he disappeared, leaving a tatty rug covering the ground where he'd been.

As I crept back down the tunnel, careful to make as little sound as possible, I thought over what I had heard. It seemed humans (from our group?) had been here and taken care of the other mice. These two had survived, somehow. Perhaps by hiding under the trap door. If there were only two of them left, we had a chance. I didn't want to underestimate them. They might have abilities I wasn't aware of, but I felt sure the five of us could defeat them if we hit them hard and fast.

I felt nervous but excited. As I neared the exit I started moving quicker, eager to get out of there and tell the others what I'd found. By the time I pushed past the bushes, I was running. I'd made it out alive!

The others saw me come out at full speed and immediately panicked, getting in each other's way before stumbling into the water. I didn't want to shout after them to stop in case it was heard from inside, so I chased them all the way back to the island.

25. Monster Hunter 1.0

Once I'd explained we weren't in any immediate danger and they'd calmed down, I told them what I'd seen. I used a stick to draw a rough map in the ground, showing the layout.

"That's it?" said Maurice. "Just five rooms?"

"There's also whatever's under the trap door. I figure the two of them used it to avoid being captured when the other mice were killed. If they have any treasure, that's probably where they keep it. Of course, who knows what mice consider valuable? It could just be a big lump of cheese."

"Actually," said Dudley, "mice don't really like cheese. Bread or even chocolate works better in traps. Their love of cheese is a myth."

"Thank you for that, Dudley," I said sarcastically. "Very interesting."

"You're very welcome," replied Dudley with complete sincerity.

"So you want us to go in there and kill them," said Claire. "While they're having their dinner."

"Yes. I told you what they said. They plan to attack humans as soon as reinforcements arrive — it's not like they're just minding their own business. I'm pretty sure the other groups have been through here and that's how they got enough money together to leave Probet. Took all the weapons and whatever else they could sell. But if they didn't know about the trap door, we might still get lucky."

"So what's the plan?" asked Maurice.

"Very simple. Two of them, five of us. They won't be prepared, and we will be ruthless. It's very important we don't give them any sort of chance. Each of us will have a role, and you have to do your part or we'll end up being the ones getting killed." I looked at Claire. "If you really don't want to do this, then stay out here. If you go in, you have to stay focused on the objective and follow it through to the end, no matter what." I looked around the group. "No matter what."

They agreed and were convinced by me that we would be victorious. I, on the other hand, had some doubts.

Even though it seemed a fairly uneven match in our favour, you can never overlook the ability of an idiot to fuck things up. And I had four of them to contend with. Who am I kidding? Five, if you include me. I was just as likely to have a panic attack at exactly the wrong moment and cost us the win. But I thought back to Maurice and Dudley making sure not to get the sacks wet when they jumped in the water. They were capable of living up to expectations, even going beyond them, sometimes at least. I just hoped this was one of those times.

We made our way to the cave entrance, weapons ready. The plan was simple. We rush in, the girls would grab the female mouse and keep hold of her. They didn't have to kill her, just keep her out of the picture while we dealt with the male. Maurice and Dudley would take an arm each, I would go in for the kill with my spike. Being able to talk made them superior beasts, which meant if I used my spike to kill one of them, I'd have completed my agreement with the blacksmith's apprentice. The others didn't know that, of course, they just thought I was willing to take on the burden of dealing the killing blow. Which I was.

We entered the tunnel and quickly moved to the other end. As arranged, the others hid in the openings, two on each side, while I sidled along the wall to make sure the mice were where they were supposed to be. They were sat around the fire with their backs to me. I signalled the others to come forward, ready to attack.

Okay, quick show of hands, who thinks things went according to plan, all nice and smooth? Nobody? Excellent, nice to see you're starting to understand how my life works.

We charged in. As instructed, no one made a sound. No yelling or threats. Why alert them to our presence before we land the first hit? The girls jumped on the female and pinned her to the ground, squealing (all three of them).

Maurice rugby tackled the male but couldn't keep hold of him, sending him skidding along the ground. He scrambled to get away, but I managed to grab his foot and yank him back. Maurice and Dudley threw themselves on an arm each. I took out my spike and closed in.

The mouse kicked and struggled violently, bucking to get free. His tail whipped around in a frenzy making it hard for me to strike. I grabbed the tail and pulled it aside and kneeled on the mouse's stomach, hand raised with the spike pointed at his face. Its eyes darted from side to side, panic welling up as its struggles were firmly restrained.

Flossie screamed. The female mouse had got free of Claire and had buried its teeth in Flossie's thigh. Dudley let go of the arm he had been holding, and rushed over to help Flossie.

"No," I yelled, "don't—"

Too late. The mouse used its free hand to punch Maurice in the face, knocking him away, I lunged, trying to stab the mouse. It twisted out of the way, got its tail free of my grip and wrapped it around my throat.

I desperately tried to get it off, but it was wrapped around tight, squeezing. My head felt like it was going to explode.

Maurice tackled the mouse again, and it released me to get away. It scrambled to the other side of the room, moving amazingly fast. I sat up wheezing and gasping for breath. Dudley had got the female mouse off Flossie and was helping her up. The mouse-woman was in the corner, hissing and snarling.

The male mouse came running out of a dark corner with a spear held in front of it, levelled at Maurice. He dived out of the way.

My head spun, my whole body was shaking and my throat felt like it was on fire. I groggily got to my feet, stumbled forward a few steps, and then ran.

Down the tunnel. Past the bushes. Into the water.

I climbed onto the island and lay on my back, gasping for breath. I was livid. Fuck them.

I sat up and saw them wading through the water. Dudley was helping Flossie. Claire and Maurice were each checking the other was okay. Fuck all of them.

I got back in the water and headed for the opposite side. Hopefully, the bunnicorns had gone back to the clearing or wherever. I got out of the water and leaned against a tree wanting to scream.

Behind me, they had continued past the island probably thinking I wanted to put some extra distance between me and the danger. I did, but the danger I wanted to get away from was them.

"What the fuck?" I yelled at them as they staggered out of the water, sopping wet. "What the actual fucking fuck?"

Everyone looked down, red-faced and unsure of what to say.

Except for Dudley, who looked up at the sky. "Colin, I —"

"What, Dudley? I'm sorry? I'm useless? I'm a total retard who almost got everyone killed?"

"He didn't get anyone killed," Claire shouted back at me. "He saved Flossie."

"He didn't save anyone. She got bitten. If the mouse had

rabies it's already too late for her, otherwise she'll be fine." I turned to Dudley who had his mouth half open. "And if you tell me mice don't carry rabies, I will stab you in the heart, so shut up. Fucking one thing, just one thing you had to do. Stay focused. But you can't help yourself, can you? This is why you've always disappointed people. You want to be a free spirit? Great, do whatever the fuck you want. Keeping your word obviously means nothing to you, and next time you're going to get someone killed. Probably me."

"That's enough," said Claire.

"Damn right it is. Piss off, all of you."

"I-I'm sorry," stammered Dudley. "I know I let you down. It's just, I-I—"

"What? It's not your fault? You meant well? It doesn't matter. Next time will be the same because no one ever taught you the importance of doing what you promised. My life's been full of people like you. '*I meant it at the time, but things change...*" That's not how it works. You're either someone who can keep their word, or you're a fucking liar. I can't rely on you, Dudley, so I think it's best I just rely on myself."

Dudley clenched both fists by his side and lowered his head to look me in the eye. "Then teach me."

"Teach you what?"

"Teach me how to do what needs to be done. If you're so f-f-fucking perfect, teach me. I'll do whatever you say."

We glared at each other for what seemed like forever and then I said, "Fine."

And so began the training of Dudley Fenderson III.

26. Teach Me, Master

If you're expecting an intense series of life changing experiences bookended by Dudley struggling around an assault course at the start, and flying around the same course to the theme from *Rocky* at the end, I'm afraid you're going to be disappointed.

I didn't have time to rebuild Dudley from the ground up, and even if I did, changing him from upper class twit to stone cold killer was well beyond me. My only goal was to get him to focus on one thing at a time so that when I told him to do something, I had confidence he would actually do it. With a normal person, you'd just say, "Look, I want you to do this thing, and it's important, really important, so don't stop until it's finished. No matter what happens, this is your number one priority. We're all counting on you, okay?" And the person would understand.

That kind of approach wouldn't work with Dudley. He would certainly agree to the task, but once he got distracted (by Flossie, by a passing bird, by the sound of his stomach rumbling...) he'd forget what he was supposed to be doing. I needed a way to demonstrate what 'important' actually meant.

"I want you to pile these on top of each other." I placed a handful of small stones in front of him. They were my collection of shots for my sling. I had selected the flattest ones, ten in all.

Dudley kneeled down next to me. "You want me to build a tower?"

"Exactly. And while you try to do that, I'm going to distract you. Whatever I say or do, I want you to ignore me and stay focused on building the tower. Nothing else matters. Understand?"

He nodded and lined up the stones on the ground.

I stood up and positioned myself on one side of him. "Ready? Go."

Dudley put the first stone on top of another, carefully balancing it for maximum stability.

I leaned forward so my mouth was close to his ear and started screaming at him. "You fucking piece of shit, I hope you die!"

Dudley knocked over the two-stone tower and recoiled from me, a look of shock on his face.

"What? I said I was going to try and distract you. You're supposed to ignore me, remember?" I could see the concept of what I was trying to do take root in his brain, like a mushroom growing in the crack of a dead tree. This was the only way to make him actually get it. Now the door was open, I just had to kick him through. "Let's try again."

He nodded, got back into position and waited for me.

"Okay, go." He put the second stone on the first, the third stone on the second. "You're useless! You've always been useless. No one likes you because there's nothing good about you."

I was yelling in his ear at full volume. Full on abuse with no pauses. And I had plenty to say.

"The world would be infinitely improved if you didn't exist. Your mother would abort you now if she had the chance, you fucking failure!"

Dudley's hands were shaking. He had stacked five stones on top of each other before they tumbled down.

"Again! Keep going, you loser. Don't wait for me to tell you — start again. If you haven't accomplished the goal, you keep trying. Holy shit, you dumb fuck, that was only four that time. Again. Again. Hurry up. Stop listening to me and focus. Do you want to be this hopeless for the rest of your life? Don't look at me, these questions are rhetorical, you arse-wipe, look at what you're doing. Quicker!"

I kept it up for ten minutes before my voice started getting hoarse. Dudley managed to get to seven stones but he was shaking all over and breathing hard from the pummelling. I straightened up, my back aching, and stretched.

"Maurice, take over."

The others were sat watching, a mixture of embarrassment and concern on their faces. Maurice hesitantly came over and took my place.

"Remember," I said to Dudley. "it doesn't matter what he says, ignore it and complete the task."

I nodded at Maurice. He exchanged an apologetic look with Dudley, and then launched into it with a surprising amount of gusto.

"You miserable maggot! What do you think this is, a holiday. Get on with it. Do it. Do it. Do it. I hate you. Your mother hates you. God hates you. Jesus died for your sins, you piece of garbage. Not my sins, not anyone else's sins, just yours. You will go to Hell, you and Hitler, no one else. Him for being an evil bastard, and you for just being you."

I was impressed. The religious angle was a nice touch. Dudley at least seemed to have stopped taking everything personally and was able to concentrate on building his tower, although he still hadn't got past seven stones.

"Can I have a word with you?" said Claire.

"What?"

"No, in private."

Reluctantly, I followed her. She stopped behind some trees and crossed her arms, her face full of frowns. "Look, I know you're doing this for a reason," she said in a forced whisper, "but you don't have to be so cruel."

"Yes, I do," I whispered back. "I'm not making him do

this. If he wants to stop, he can. It's up to him, not you."

"I know that, but he's trying his best, we all are."

"No, you're not. You know how you know when you're trying your best? You feel terrible. Your body hurts all over, you're exhausted, you can't think straight, you want to give up but you keep going, hating every minute. It's horrible. That's why nobody does it. It's much easier to not try your best and just say you did. The way you're saying it now."

Claire clenched her jaw and made a weird little grunt. "I don't know how to talk to you. Everything you say makes me want to punch you in the face."

I shrugged. "I don't know what your problem is. I've told you from the start, you can all pick up and leave any time. Walk off hand in hand and go make friendship bracelets for each other as you slowly starve to death. My only advice would be, if you do resort to cannibalism, eat Dudley first."

I returned to Dudley hunched over his tower of stones and Maurice running out of steam.

"Welsh people don't like you. French people don't like you. German people do like you, which is even worse."

"Flossie, your turn," I said.

Flossie, who had been massaging the bite she'd received — thanks to her rough hessian trousers, it hadn't even pierced the skin, just left a red mark — looked up at me in horror.

"Ah can't."

"We have to show him it's not personal. If only some of us do it, it'll look like me and Maurice really hate him." Complete bollocks, of course. I just wanted to see what she'd come up with.

Flossie slowly got to her feet and walked over to swap places with Maurice. "What do I do?"

"Just distract him. Dudley, you're nearly there. This

time." I gave him a thumbs up, which only confused him. "Okay, go."

Dudley started stacking. Flossie stood there frozen for a moment, then spun around so her back was to him and started singing.

"Look at mah bum. Look at mah bum. Look at mah big, big bum." She was jumping up and down and slapping her own backside as she sang. "Look at mah bum. Look at mah bum. Look at mah big, big bum."

Dudley's whole body shook. He was bent over the rocks, a twisted knot of focus, but three, four stones and the tower would topple.

"Look at mah bum. Look at mah bum. Look at mah big, big bum."

"Don't you fucking look, Dudley. Keep going. Nothing else matters."

Sweat was pouring off his face. Tom Cruise deciding whether to cut the green or yellow wire couldn't even come close to this scene for pure intensity.

Flossie was getting into her little song and dance, wiggling and jiggling as she sang. "Look at mah bum. Look at mah bum. Look at mah big, big bum."

Dudley got up to nine stones before they fell, quite an achievement. He leaned back with his eyes tightly closed, and roared at the sky. "Arghhh! It's not fair! I want to see her big, sexy bum!"

Flossie stopped and turned around, her face flushed beetroot-red.

Dudley opened his eyes and looked at her. She made a 'yeep' sound and ran away.

"What?" Dudley looked at the rest of us. "Where is she going?"

Claire headed off after Flossie. "It's alright, I'll get her. I don't think anyone's called her bum sexy before."

"That was good Dudley. You did well."

He looked disappointed. "I didn't do all ten."

"I'm surprised you got to nine," I said. "I tried it before I gave them to you. Couldn't get past six."

27. Monster Hunter 2.0

As we waited for the girls to come back, Dudley continued to try and stack the stones even though no one told him to and we weren't shouting at him any more. He just wanted to do it. Once an idea took hold in that brain of his, it really took hold.

"So," said Maurice, "we going back in there, then?"

I nodded. "They'll be ready for us this time, but I think we can still take them. That spear he had looked pretty nasty, but he could hardly hold it. If we rush him, I don't think he'll be able to stop us."

"Yeah, yeah," said Maurice. "There was something else I wanted to ask you. About Claire."

I turned to face him. "Oh? What?"

"Is there something going on between you two? Just wondering, you know, because you're always at each other's throats. If this was movie, the couple that's always fighting are the ones who end up together at the end, right?"

"If this was a romantic comedy, maybe. But this more like a horror movie. Believe me, there's nothing going on. Why? Are you interested in her?"

"Who me? No. No, of course not. I mean, I'm probably not her type." He pushed his glasses up his nose and I'm pretty sure he was blushing, although it's hard to tell with black people who have very dark skin like him. And no, that's not racist.

Claire and Flossie returned, and I told everyone we were going to try again. They looked a bit apprehensive, but no one objected. Flossie had calmed down but was smiling more than normal, although I couldn't tell if she was pleased at being told she had a sexy bum or grinning out of embarrassment. Maybe a bit of both. We made our way back to the cave and prepared ourselves once more.

I pointed my finger at Dudley. "This time, get hold of the guy and don't let go. Doesn't matter what happens to the rest of us, that's your only job."

Dudley nodded, his face a picture of earnest determination.

I turned to the others. "Ready?"

"Hold on," said Maurice and he started fiddling with the collar of his onesie. I've mentioned before that it had a Batman theme, although it wasn't made to look like a costume, it just had lots of bat insignia printed on it. So it was a bit of a surprise when Maurice unzipped part of the collar and pulled out a hood. Or should I say cowl. With little bat ears.

It covered most of his face and the eye holes didn't quite match where his eyes were, although when he put his glasses back on, they sort of held the mask in place.

"Right," he said in a low growl. "Let's do this."

I didn't say anything. I was just thankful he didn't want to wear one of the blankets as a cape.

We stormed into the tunnel and ran all the way down. We burst into the end room, ready for battle, to find it completely empty.

This wasn't completely unexpected. I had told them about the trapdoor, and when I went over to the rug — a large mat woven out of reeds — and pointed at it, they all understood. I bent down and whisked the rug away, to reveal... the ground. No trapdoor, no sign of any kind of entrance.

I got down on my knees and looked closer. I brushed away the dirt to try and find any edges or a hidden handle. Nothing.

"Are you sure it was there?" asked Maurice.

"Definitely."

Was it a magic door? Or just really well hidden? I went over to the fire, which was still burning away, and picked up the pot hanging over it. The contents were a fishy stew. I returned to where I had seen the trapdoor and poured out the contents of the pot.

The steaming liquid spread out and then sank into invisible crevices, showing the outline of the door and a flat circular handle. I was about to yank it open, but before I had a chance, the door flew open, and with a yell the old mouse leapt out of the hole carrying the spear.

I'm not sure how good real mice are at jumping — Dudley obviously would know, but I didn't want to distract him — but the mouse-man was out in one bound. He waved the spear at us. It was too big for him to hold properly, so the end drooped, but it could still inflict a nasty wound, so no one wanted to get too close.

"You will all die here," he squeaked. "Death is your reward for attacking the innocent." Behind him, the female mouse had emerged and held onto his shoulder, like she was lining him up.

It made me feel a bit awkward to hear him talk. A wild beast was one thing, but this was an actual person. We all stood around, unsure how to proceed.

"Listen to me," said the mouse. "I am prepared to allow you to leave. We are peace-loving people. If you leave us alone, we will leave you alone."

"I heard you, before," I said. "You were planning to attack us as soon as more of your men arrive. You aren't peace-loving."

The mouse jabbed his spear at me. "Only to defend ourselves! We were attacked in our sleep by your people. Slaughtered. We will find those cowards and deliver justice. That is our right."

He had a point. Were we really heroes fighting monsters here? It didn't feel like it. I lowered my spike.

"Now!" screamed the mouse. The female behind him threw out some kind of dust that filled the air. My eyes stung, making it hard to see. I heard the others call out in pain. Then, almost too late, I saw the spear coming right at me. I lurched sideways, so it went between my body and arm and grabbed hold of the shaft. A push-pull struggle ensued.

Batman, of course, was unaffected. Not because of the outfit, but because he wore glasses. Maurice jumped in and shoved the female. Through blurry vision I saw her suddenly disappear. Not by magic, she had fallen down the hole.

The mouse turned to check on her, and I yanked the spear out of his grasp. Dudley swooped in. He grabbed the mouse from behind, wrapping his arm around the creature's tiny throat, and lifted him off the ground. I moved in, wiping away tears with my sleeve.

The madly kicking feet and whipping tail made it hard to get close, so I kicked it between the legs hoping to hit mouse balls, assuming he had them. I must have hit something, or maybe winded him, because he stopped struggling. I dived in and started stabbing. My vision was still blurred and my aim was a bit wild, so I hit Dudley's arm a couple of times. He didn't let go.

I could feel the spike enter the mouse's head, strike against the skull, push through to its brain. After five or six direct hits, the mouse went limp. I retreated, breathing hard. The girls were still trying to see straight, most of the dust had gone in their direction.

Maurice picked up the fallen spear and walked over to the hole just as the female mouse jumped out screaming, something held aloft in her hand. Instinctively, Maurice thrust the spear forward and sent the tip straight into her open mouth and out the other side. She fell to the floor. The thing in her hand was a rock.

Maurice dropped his end of the spear, which was stuck in the mouse's mouth. He looked stunned. Dudley was still holding the male mouse in a vice-like grip, taking his newly learned lesson to heart.

"You can let go now, Dudley," I said.

He nodded, and the dead mouse slumped into a heap next to the female. We had won. Or at least, we hadn't died, which was a victory in itself. Now, someone had to go down the hole and claim our reward.

28. Loot Roll

Everyone stood around trying not to look at the bodies of the mice. We'd managed to keep going on pure adrenalin during the fight, but now it all looked very real, and very much like a crime scene.

"Dudley, you know the washing line outside? Pull it down and bring it in here. Maurice, go get the sacks from the island. Claire, take Flossie to the pond and wash her eyes out, she looks like she's still got some of the dust in there. I'll take care of this." I pointed at the bodies without looking at them.

They all stood still for a moment — I thought they were going to have a go at me for trying to boss them around — but they turned and went off as instructed. I didn't particularly feel like giving orders, but they needed to stop dwelling on what we'd just done, and I think they were glad to have something to do. The other reason for my sudden take-charge attitude was that I really needed to be alone.

As soon as they'd gone, I sat on the ground with a bump and burst into tears. I know, just when you think I couldn't get any more manly. It wasn't really crying, more shuddering sobs that lasted for about ten seconds and that was it. I think my body just needed to get it out.

Once it was over, I stood up feeling calm. No, not calm, numb. An emotion I welcomed.

Getting the spear out of the female mouse's head was a nightmare. It wouldn't come out the way it had entered, so I had to push it all the way through and pull it out the other end. Even more horrible than it sounds.

I put the bodies next to each other. Dudley came in carrying the rope with laundry still attached. I took the cloths and laid them over the mice, not out of respect, just so we wouldn't have to look at them.

The others arrived a few moments later. The atmosphere was pretty wretched, and they were all waiting for me to tell them what to do. I took a torch out of the sack and lit it off the fire. It burnt quite well, although I could tell it wouldn't last long. I had a look down the hole. It was deeper than I'd expected, although wide enough to allow me down. Someone smaller would probably have an easier time, but I couldn't see either of the girls volunteering.

Before I attempted it, I did a quick survey of the other rooms. They had been too dark to search before, but now I had the torch. I didn't bother explaining what I was doing, the others just followed.

The rooms were all empty apart from straw bedding against each wall. There were also dark splotches on the floor and walls. I guessed they were blood splatters from when the mice were killed, but I didn't say anything.

The last room we checked had a broken lantern in it. This was the source of the glass I had cut myself on. A lantern would be more useful than the torch (which was already spluttering its last). I stuck the torch inside the lantern as best I could, and the wick caught light. I could feel liquid splosh around inside the base, but without glass the light wasn't very bright. But bright enough.

I assumed it ran on oil, although where you got oil from, I had no idea.

We returned to the hole. Dudley and Maurice held onto one end of the rope and lowered me down. I was relieved when I hit bottom — I had been worried the rope wouldn't be long enough. There was a tunnel leading away, but I had to get on my hand and knees to enter it. I'm not claustrophobic, but squeezing myself through made my scalp tingle and my heart palpitate. With all the craziness going on, I had forgotten what a wuss I was. I tried to calm myself and forced myself forward. The tunnel narrowed even more, so I had to crawl on my stomach, pushing the lantern ahead of me. I could taste dirt in my mouth and feel the walls tighten around me.

I finally reached the end, and it opened into a small cavern, large enough for me to sit up. In a corner there was a roll of parchment. What was it? A treasure map? A magic scroll? I unrolled it.

A piece of charcoal fell out. The page was covered in drawings. Quite realistic poses of the female mouse, on her back, legs open showing her privates. In detail. A lot of close-up detail.

After a few moments of trying to make sense of what I was looking at, I started laughing. What an idiot. I had come to a strange fantastical world and turned myself into someone prepared to kill for porn. The other could probably hear my maniacal laughter and must have thought I'd gone insane. Maybe I had.

I left the mouse porn in the little cave and made my way back out. Going up was a lot harder than coming down, but with Maurice and Dudley pulling me up, I finally returned to the surface, panting and sweating, covered in dirt.

"Did you find anything?" asked Maurice.

"No, nothing. We should get back. And we'll have to take them with us." I pointed to the covered mice.

"Do we really have to?" asked Claire.

"Yes. I don't know what they're worth, but I'm not skinning them. We still need money though, unless you want to eat more turd-bunnies."

That thought was enough to convince them to grit their teeth and just do it.

We bound the mice up in their cloth shrouds and grabbed an end each. The female turned out to be heavier than the male, so me and Dudley took her. The other three carried the male by pushing the spear through the rope bindings and lifting it, with Maurice at one end and the girls at the other.

It was later afternoon when we set off around the pond with two dead mice and a broken lantern. If that had been my reward for a quest in an RPG, I think I would have uninstalled the game. Sadly, I didn't have that option.

It was only when we reached the clearing that I remembered the bunnicorns. The last thing we needed was to be attacked by them. I signalled the others to stop and crept forward to see if they were still about.

They were. The clearing was full of them, lying on their backs, snuggling with each other. Whatever disagreements they'd had, they seemed to have sorted them out.

Very quietly, we skirted the edge of the clearing and found our way out of the forest. Despite my concerns, it was fairly easy to recognise the way we'd come, the marks we'd left on the trees providing reassurance we were going in the right direction, but that was all.

Out in the open, with a gentle breeze cooling us off, I was able to relax a little. I hadn't realised how tense I had become until then. We could have taken a break, but no one wanted to stop.

By the time we reached Probet, the light was starting to fade. I headed for the shed. If Grayson was still there, I had some questions to ask him, finally.

29. Behind the Curtain

There was a cart and horse outside the shed. It was the first horse we'd seen. It looked like a regular horse, no wings or horns. Soldiers were piling sacks and boxes into the back while Grayson watched. He saw us approach, and his eyebrows rose.

"Ah, you're back. Looks like you've been busy. What have you got there?"

We dumped the bodies in front of him.

"First, I want to ask you about this." I took the bunnicorn horn out of one of the sacks and showed it to him. He jerked back like I was offering him a severed penis.

"Why," he asked, "are you holding that severed penis?"

I looked down at my hand. "No, this is a horn from a rabbit."

"Yes," said Grayson, "a rabbit penis. When it's their mating season, they incubate inside an ogre and come out with the horn."

I stared at the thing in my hand unable to work out what to do with it. How do you dispose of a severed penis? If I had access to the internet, I'm sure I'd have thirty million search results to that question.

"But they all had them. There weren't any females." That's all I could think, still trying to convince myself I wasn't holding a cock in my hand.

"They are both male and female. Once they get the horn, they form a circle and, well, I won't go into the details. I wouldn't carry that around if I were you. You'll scare the children."

I turned around and threw it as hard as I could. It sailed over the buildings and out of sight. I turned back and pretended the last few minutes had never happened.

"Can you have a look at these and tell us if we did the right thing?" I pointed at the mice.

He bent down and unwrapped the cloth over the male mouse's face. He stared at me open-mouthed. "You did this?"

I nodded.

He rushed towards me, grabbed my shoulders and shook me. "Well done, my boy, well done. You have done us a great service."

"We have?" I was relieved he saw it as a good thing, but a little confused at the enthusiasm of his response.

"This isn't just an ordinary mouse warrior — although that would have been a worthy achievement too — this is their king. Every nest only has one breeding pair, the mouse king and its mate. You can kill off all their warriors, and this little monster will repopulate the colony in a few weeks. They're incredibly hard to kill. They stay hidden most of the time."

He bent down and undid the other mouse's wrapping. "And you got the female too! This is wonderful."

He pulled apart the cloth until the female was fully exposed. Seeing her lifeless body again put a knot in my stomach, and I turned to the others. They were all avoiding looking at it. Grayson, on the other hand, poked the body with a gleeful look on his face.

"Seems like you got her just in time. She was pregnant. A few days at most before she would have birthed a litter of at least four or five."

The tightness in my stomach fell away, like I was going downhill on a rollercoaster. My throat constricted, so my voice sounded strange to my ears. "We didn't know." A cold shiver ran through me, and sweat broke out on my face.

The replacement mice they were expecting weren't

reinforcements from some other nest, it was their babies.

Grayson looked up at me. "There's no need to be shocked. These weren't babes you need to regret ridding us of. In six months they would have grown into mature males. There's only one breeding pair in the nest, so the males find their jollies elsewhere. That means they kidnap young girls from places like this town and use them to satisfy their urges. We sometimes find the bodies, or what's left of them. Let me tell you, you should be enormously proud of yourselves."

I was still reeling from what he'd said. Even though he made a compelling case for killing them, I still couldn't get rid of the feeling we had done something horrific. Claire had her hand over her mouth. Flossie's mouth was grinning, but her eyes were filled with desperation. Dudley, as usual, found solace in the skies. And Maurice, who had been the one to kill the female, stared at the ground, his shoulders slumped. No one felt proud.

"Come with me," said Grayson as he stood up. "I need to give you your reward. Fenner, go tell the Mayor the mouse king has been killed. Jerrick, Carten, put the bodies in the cart, we'll take them with us."

The soldiers all rushed into action as we followed Grayson into the shed in a daze.

Grayson headed over to the desk and opened a drawer. He took out a bunch of books.

"The bounty on the king is substantial. I don't have enough money here, but I can give you a chit you can cash in when you get to the city."

"Bounty?" I said.

"Mm? Oh, yes." Grayson walked over to the curtain and pulled it open.

The wall was covered in posters. Each had a picture of a creature on it, some writing I couldn't understand and a number. They were wanted posters. Each was a different colour. I looked over at the map on the other wall and noticed for the first time that parts of it were in different colours. By matching the colours of the posters to the map, you could tell where each creature could be found.

I couldn't take it all in. What did it mean? Why hadn't he told us about this?

The poster with a mouse on it had the number 100 on it.

"The mouse is worth a 100 chobs?" I asked.

Grayson opened one of the books and started writing in it. "Oh no. A regular mouse warrior is 100 bits. But the mouse king, that's a special reward. 500 bits."

After scrabbling around trying to get a few chobs together, suddenly we had 500 bits.

"And then there's the female. That's another 300. Plus she's pregnant, that's another 500. All together, that's 1300 bits. All I have is a hundred bits left, your friends cleaned me out I'm afraid, but if you take this and hand it in at the Municipal Directory — every city has one — they'll be able to convert it into cash for you." He ripped the page out of the book and handed it to me.

It had some words on it, his signature and the number 1200. He then put ten red coins in a small pouch and gave it to me.

I took them from him, but I wasn't really aware of what I was doing. I kept looking at all the different posters.

"I don't understand. Why didn't you tell us about this before? When you first explained everything, you could have said something."

"I know it may seem unnecessarily unhelpful, but experience has shown us that the best way to help visitors like yourselves is to let you search for answers rather than just giving them to you. If we offer too much assistance, you'll become dependent on us. This is the way it's been for a hundred years — the system works, trust me. Your friends were able to figure things out. You're group was, ah, a little slow getting there. But here you are."

"Slow?" The numbness had dissipated. All I felt now was rage. "Of course we were slow. Look at us! We didn't ask to come here. You forced us to do horrible things and then kept information from us to make it even harder."

"I'm sorry. I have my orders."

The old 'I was just following orders excuse'. This world really wasn't all that different to ours. I pointed at the posters. "Can you at least tell us what they say?"

He shook his head. "I'm afraid not. Another thing you need to work out. I can, however give you this." He gave me one of the books on his desk.

I opened it. There were pictures in it. An apple on the first page, a ball on the second, a cat on the third... a basic kid's learn to read book.

"We don't have time to learn your language now. Just read them for us."

Grayson shook his head. "That's not how it works."

I stepped up to him, hardly able to contain myself. "Just fucking do it."

He didn't move. His face showed no signs of caring about my demands. Until, that is, he felt the sword poking him in the stomach.

Wait. Sword? Where did I get a sword? I was wondering that myself, but I definitely had a sword in my hand. It was Grayson's, and I had taken it from its scabbard without him realising. And without me realising either.

I had seen Grayson in action. He was strong and fast, and knew how to handle himself. If he had sensed me going for his weapon, I have no doubt he'd have been able to stop me. But he didn't see it coming because I had no idea I was going to do it. My body did it without my permission, and you can't read a person's intention if they don't have any.

Grayson's face didn't have that irritating smile on it for once. For a pro like him to get disarmed by a noob must have been infuriating. He was probably planning six different ways to kill me, but I was all in, and it was too late to worry about little things like dying.

I pointed at the wall of posters. "Read."

30. Farewell to Probet

Of all the things you might force someone to do by pointing a sword at them, reading probably isn't one that immediately springs to mind. I pointed at the posters on the wall, each with a line of something unintelligible written on them.

"I said read it."

Grayson stood with his hands held up, more requesting calm than offering surrender. "Now, you don't want to — argh."

I only meant to poke him slightly with the sword to show him I meant business, but the tip slid into his side with ease. I pulled it back out, a red smear on the end. So this was how a real weapon worked.

Grayson started reading. "Ogre, easily confused, 300 bits. Frogman, uses basic beast magic, 200 bits. Gnome, weak to bright light, 100 bits. Lamia, able to mesmerise, 250 bits."

"Maurice, grab some paper and write this stuff down. Claire, you get some paper too and copy the map off the wall. Mark where the different creatures live. The colour of the poster matches the same colour region on the map."

They quickly did as told. Grayson continued reading out the names of different mythical beasts (apparently not as mythical as I had been taught to believe) and their weaknesses/abilities. Maurice scribbled everything down. A cheat sheet.

I held the sword pointed at Grayson, although I felt like he was letting me. If he had rushed me, I doubt I could have stopped him from taking his sword back.

It took about ten minutes to get all the information jotted down. Some of the monsters I'd heard of, others were new to me. Grayson had one hand on his waist, stemming the flow of blood. It wasn't spraying out or anything, but it did look painful. I had an urge to ask him if he was okay, even to apologise, but it would seem a bit disingenuous, seeing as how I was the one that had wounded him.

"Okay," I said, "let's go."

We backed away from him, heading for the exit. Grayson didn't say anything, didn't call for help from his men outside. It occurred to me we would be fugitives from now on. Outlaws. I really didn't want to be on the run for the rest of my days (not that there'd be many of those the way we were going).

I looked at the sword in my hand. It was a beautifully crafted weapon, even I who knew nothing could tell that.

"This sword probably means a lot to you. I don't really want to take it from you. If I leave it here, will you give me your word you won't come after us?"

Grayson looked surprised, but he nodded. I place the sword on the bench nearest the door.

"Will you be reporting us for this?"

"For showing some initiative? No. But if we cross paths again..."

He left it hanging, but I got the idea. Keep paths uncrossed. We had made it to the door and were about to leave when Grayson said, "Wait. You're going to need this."

He opened one of the desk drawers and grimaced as he awkwardly took out another piece of card. He had to swap hands to write, grabbing his side with his free hand and picking up the charcoal stick with the one now painted red. After writing something on the card, he walked towards us.

We all flinched and took a step back. He stopped, placed the card on a bench and backed off. I took a few steps forward and picked it up. A white card with writing on it.

"They don't allow strangers into cities without one of those. It confirms you are visitors with full privileges. No tax, no tolls. The closest city is Fengarad to the west, but it will work in any of them. Show it to the guards at the gate and they should let you through without problem."

"Thank you." I didn't know what else to say. Even though I had threatened and wounded him, he was still willing to help us. That is assuming the card didn't read, *'The person holding this card is a criminal, lock him up immediately.'* I really had to learn their stupid language.

We walked out of the shed and immediately found ourselves facing the soldiers waiting by the cart. The one I had spoken to earlier in the day saluted me. Turned out all you needed to gain respect in this place was to commit mass murder.

He looked like he was going to say something, but I didn't want to hang around making small talk while Grayson changed his mind and had us all strung up by the neck.

"Right!" I said in an authoritative voice. "Evening training session starts now. Everyone keep up with me." And then I ran through the town as fast as I could with the others chasing me.

We didn't stop until we were well out of town. It was getting dark, and we needed to find somewhere to make camp. There was a small group of trees off the main road that provided cover and hid us from sight. Building a fire didn't take long, but we didn't have any food and only a little water.

"Wait here, I have to do something."

"Where are you going?" asked Claire. She seemed concerned I was going to run off.

"I have some unfinished business in town. I won't be

long. Here." I handed the chit for 1200 bits to Maurice. "Hang onto that. And take this too." I gave him the pouch with the money in it, but first I took out a handful of coins. "I'll try to bring back some food."

"Do you want one of us to come with you?" said Dudley.

"No, it'll be easier for me to sneak in and out by myself. Don't worry, I won't take any risks, trust me."

And they did trust me. Which was fine, because I was trustworthy. For now, anyway.

I walked back into town keeping a low profile and avoiding any people that were about. Flaming torches outside each store were the only form of light and provided plenty of shadows for me to sneak through on my way to the smithy.

The blacksmith was banging away as I approached. He glanced up, didn't seem very impressed, and went back to banging. I stood in front of him, but I was here to see someone else. Kizwat came out to a backroom carrying a box of something. He stopped when he saw me.

"Kizwat, I need to speak to you."

This got the blacksmith's attention. He put his hammer down, wiped his hands on his leather apron and turned to look at his apprentice. "What's this about, Kizwat?"

Kizwat shrugged and looked at me. He seemed worried I was going to make things awkward for him somehow. He was sort of right.

"I killed the Mouse King."

"That was you?" said Kizwat, his eyes wide with surprise. "We heard the news, but I didn't imagine..."

"Yes, well, me neither. But I used this to do it." I held up the spike he had made for me. "I'm assuming the Mouse King counts as a superior beast?"

Kizwat's mouth fell open, and he dropped the box he was holding. It clanged as it hit the floor. He shook his head. "No, he doesn't." His voice was small and weak.

"Really? But he spoke, doesn't that mean..."

"The Mouse King isn't a superior beast," said the blacksmith. His demeanour had changed from disinterest to intense irritation. "The Mouse King is a unique beast."

"Oh. Is that better? I mean, you can still get your hammer, right?"

Kizwat, still stunned, nodded. He looked to his master with a goofy smile on his face.

"You made this weapon?" the blacksmith asked him.

"Yes, master. I made it from an off-cut, using the spinning technique you taught me." He turned to me. "A unique beast means I will be able to claim a silver hammer. I'll be able to open my own forge. People will come from all around to buy what I make. A silver grade blacksmith is very rare."

I never expected to kill a superior beast in the first place, let alone something even rarer. "In that case, maybe we should amend our deal."

Kizwat nodded vigorously. "Whatever you want me to make, at cost price."

The blacksmith's mood didn't improve. "Did you really use *that* to make the killing blow? They have ways of verifying these things. Don't send my apprentice all the way to the Guild on a hoax."

"Unlikely as it might seem, it's the truth. His blood is still on here."

"You must have got lucky," said the blacksmith.

"Yes," I agreed.

Kizwat walked over to me. He looked nervous and sweaty. "I'll need to take the weapon. I'll have to show it to the Guild Master."

I gave him the spike, a little reluctantly. I hadn't realised I'd have to return it. "I don't suppose you could make me another one?"

"Wait here," said the blacksmith. He disappeared into

the back.

"Where will you set up your forge?" I asked Kizwat. "If you're to make good on our deal, I need to be able to find you."

Kizwat was staring lovingly at the spike. "I will head to Dargot. It is the city in the north. They had a silver blacksmith there who died recently."

"Won't his apprentice inherit his hammer?"

"Silver hammers can't be passed down, they must be earned. Come find me there in a couple of months and I should be ready to make you whatever you wish."

Seemed like a good plan. The blacksmith returned carrying something wrapped in green cloth. He opened it to reveal a short sword, about the length of my forearm.

"Take this. The same deal you made with Kizwat. A man who gets lucky once might get lucky again."

I took the sword. It wasn't as flash as Grayson's, but it had the same feel. A real weapon.

"Agreed. I will come back if I kill another unique beast." Although, to be honest, I had no intention of hunting any more monsters. Defending myself from other humans, however, would probably always be a thing.

"Or maybe something higher," said the blacksmith.

"Higher than a unique beast? There's something like that?"

"Indeed. A very unique beast."

I couldn't help but scoff a little. "If unique means there's only one of them, what does very unique mean?"

"There is only one unique beast in a group. When they die, a new one is born, eventually. A very unique beast, there is only one in all the world, and when it dies, it is gone for good. They are tremendously powerful." The blacksmith sucked in his breath. "It is unlikely you will ever encounter one, but..."

I made a mental note to avoid very unique beasts at all

costs.

On the way out of town I bought some chickens from the butcher. He also sold animal fat, which we could use to fuel the lantern. I found this out by asking, a new skill I seemed to have picked up. I also bought a proper bag and some other bits and pieces. With money in my pocket, I could have spent hours shopping, but the longer I spent in town, the more powerful the urge to get out of there got. Leaving Probet felt like the only way to truly graduate from being a noob.

I still considered it more than likely that this would turn out to be a game, but whether it was or not didn't make a difference at this point. I had to find a way to survive. Not only to be able to live, but to be able to live with myself. Killing monsters made no sense if I had to become one to do it.

I headed out of town to meet up with my party.

Roll Call

Gadget Tramp - Can disguise weapons to look like trash, because that's what they're made of.

Angry Witch - Can cast '*Lower Self-esteem*' on herself and everyone else.

Grinning Priestess - If laughter really is the best medicine, you're saved. Otherwise, say your prayers.

Slow Ranger - Uncanny ability to always know exactly where the sky is.

Batman - The hero this world neither needs nor deserves.